Flicker

The Storm Dragons' Mate
Book 2

M. Sinclair

Lost & Bound Publishing

Flicker - The Storm Dragons' Mate (Book #2)

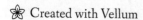 Created with Vellum

The Union of Love & Madness

Description

The most powerful and dominant shifters at DIA are my mates.

I finally shifted. I should feel relief and excitement, but instead I'm faced with fear of the unknown. The hidden threat that defeated my parents is still out there, and the looming presence of it, posing a threat to my mates, is a constant thought in the back of my mind.

As I reunite with a community I'd forgotten, I can only hope that locked away in my memories is a clue to the life that was stolen from me.

I may not be able to change the past but I'll fight to protect my future.

Flicker is book 2 in the Storm Dragons' Mate series that features a slightly naive but sassy

MFC, possessive dragon alphas, and a secret that will change everything. This is not a high school academy book and the contents are intended for mature audiences, with characters who are all 18+. This book includes violence and mature sexual content.

Author Note:

Flicker is set in the shared universe of Dark Imaginarium Academy. All series can be read independently, but characters have crossovers and it is highly encouraged to read all within the universe to understand the world in its entirety.

Series within the universe:

- Phases of the Moon by M. Sinclair
- The Creatures We Crave by R.L. Caulder
- The Storm Dragons' Mate by M. Sinclair
- Blood Oath by R.L. Caulder

Chapter One

Breaker Firespell

Something was wrong with *mo chuisle*.

We were standing right in the archway that led into the academy building's hall, our entrance currently blocked by three wolf shifters that had appeared out of nowhere, all of them seemingly freshmen. They were attempting to pick a fight with us, specifically Gage, which was something I would normally find amusing...if it wasn't stopping us from getting to Bexley. My gaze moved to the bathroom door, nearly twenty feet away, almost willing her to walk through it.

Something was very wrong here.

"Get out of my way. Now." Gage grabbed one of the wolves' collars and lifted them, his fingers morphing into claws and ripping the garment before tossing him to the side. I had a feeling that he and

1

Jagger were both feeling the same thread of panic and concern that I was.

Then I heard it—*Bexley's scream.*

I wasn't positive if I hit the kid in front of me or tossed him to the side; all I knew was that one moment I was standing in the archway at the end of the hall and the next I was throwing my full weight into the bathroom door.

A fiery blast slammed into me and nearly laid me on my ass.

It didn't stop me from pushing forward through the flames, absolute fury and red rage washing over me at what I saw.

Ioan. He had Bexley pinned to the wall, his agonizing bellow of anger making me realize he was being burned alive. Bexley's skin was glowing like hot metal, and before I had the chance to step in, she cried out as her bones snapped and her face contorted in pain.

Fuck.

I knew what came next. Attempting to shove the others back, as they had followed me in, I had a mere second to warn them. "Move—fucking move!"

Everything exploded into a lethal inferno.

I watched through the flames as Bexley transformed into the creature I knew she was meant to be, shifting into her full form. Ioan's body soared through the air with the force of her power as the entire building shook and she let out a vicious cry.

"Holy shit," Jagger breathed out, all of us watching her in absolute awe.

Without a moment of hesitation, most likely listening to the survival instincts telling her to run, Bexley exploded up and into the air, breaking right through the stone ceiling.

"We have to follow her!" Gage ordered, yelling over the sound of the debris falling around us.

I nodded sharply and jumped into the air, shifting automatically. My gold wings expanded out and pushed me through the hole in the ceiling to follow my mate. My perfect fucking mate.

I was still fucking livid at what had happened with Ioan, filled with a simmering rage that was just waiting to explode out at the right moment, but it was being grossly overshadowed by the pride, awe, and relief I felt at Bexley shifting. Her obsidian scales flashed under the sunlight as I sped after her, unable to take my gaze off her even for a minute.

Bex's movements were unsteady but fast. The burst of power from her first shift after so long wouldn't last forever, but it would be smart for us to let her ride it out. If we made her land now, she would be worked up and terrified, especially since her creature was no doubt far more in charge than herself. Instead we would let her fly, and when she was finally exhausted and decided to land...well, then we would figure out what the hell to do.

Silver and bronze forms flew on either side of me, and I knew they were thinking along the same lines because neither raced ahead to try to corral her into landing. When she made a sharp turn, most likely trying to shake us from tailing her, we followed after, easily navigating a sector we were so familiar with.

I was glad for that familiarity right now because it gave me a moment to study Bexley's true form. Of course I had seen her shift when we were younger, but she had only grown more beautiful and far more powerful. When the light hit just right, her onyx scales almost appeared to be dipped in gold on the tip, and along her spine down to her barbed tail were vertical scales that looked similar to spikes. The part of her that held most of my attention though was her *wings*.

In my life, I'd seen countless pairs of wings, but Bexley's would always remain the most beautiful in my mind. They were long and elegant, the webbing between them almost leaf-like in nature. While they were onyx-colored near her body, they faded to a light, almost transparent gold near the tips, and the veining and cartilage throughout was a stunning metallic shade. *Fucking beautiful.*

Our beautiful dragon mate.

I couldn't wait to see her up close once she landed.

We continued to let her fly for the next ten minutes, until I noticed her movements starting to slow, her wings flagging in their effort to keep her up, her elevation dipping quickly. We must have circled the back of the sector several times before she finally decided to land, making a straight line towards a series of caves in the mountains that lined the back of the sector.

I felt a thread of caution and concern as we followed, not wanting to scare her. I knew eventually that her dragon would recognize we were her mates, but her first reaction would probably be fear from being cornered by three massive male dragons. So the minute we neared the cave, I shifted back into my human form to follow her in.

The other two followed my lead.

"We need to give her some space," Jagger cautioned.

Gage looked like he wanted to argue, so I added in support, "Think how scared she probably is." He paused and nodded, but I could see the anger from the Ioan situation threatening to make him shift again. Hopefully once he saw Bexley, he would calm down a bit.

Bexley, who was hiding in the shadows of the cave, made a wounded noise that made my chest squeeze. Any anger I was still holding onto about how we'd found her in the bathroom truly disappeared, my need to take care of my mate far surpassing anything else.

"*Mo chuisle,*" I called as our eyes adjusted to the dark, finding her onyx dragon curled up as far back as possible in the cave, her dark gaze on us and her fear saturating the air. Despite not looking anything like her human form, I could *see* Bexley was there. She was terrified, confused, and probably being pulled in a million different directions by her dragon —but very much there.

"Bex," Gage called. "It's us. Gage, Jagger, and Breaker."

A threatening growl came from her throat as she curled even further in on herself.

"I promise you're safe," I said in a soft, hopefully comforting voice. "We're just here to help you shift back." I had no idea if what we were saying was the *right* thing to say, but Jagger nodded next to me in agreement.

While she didn't growl this time, she continued to stare at us with caution.

"We also need to make sure you aren't injured," Jagger added, heavy concern saturating his voice. It was completely possible she'd injured herself while busting through the ceiling. Dragons' heads were scaled and tough, but something like that would still leave a mark. And that wasn't even including what Ioan could have possibly done to hurt her—

I stopped myself from going down that train of thought. Not until Bexley was safe, healthy, and back in our dorm. Then I could entertain the fury that threatened to consume me.

Taking a chance and approaching her, she let out a threatening noise but I didn't stop my movement. When I reached the point that I was standing right in front of her, I raised my hand up, and she stared at it before leaning forward and sniffing my skin.

Bexley froze up before a softer rumble came from her throat.

When she pressed her snout against my hand, I nearly sagged, breathing out a long sigh of relief. I spoke to the others while keeping my gaze on her. "Come over here, let her scent you. I think her dragon is making it hard for her to recognize us."

Stepping slightly to the side, Jagger came up and offered his hand, her gaze moving from me to him as they repeated a similar process before Gage took his turn. I could see she was more hesitant when it came to him, and I had a feeling why.

"You have to turn the aggression down," I warned. "She can sense it."

Gage shot me a frustrated look before moving his gaze back to Bexley. "Cupcake, I promise I'm not mad or angry at you. I'm just on edge because of what happened."

Seeming to evaluate his words, or maybe his expression and intent, she finally scented him, and I watched as she visibly relaxed, her wings no longer shifting anxiously on either side of her as if preparing to fly. I knew that until she recognized all of us, or more specifically her dragon recognized us, that she would perceive us as a threat, and I couldn't blame her.

Other shifters feared us for a reason. Bexley never needed to worry about that though.

"I need you to shift back," I instructed her, her head tilting in confusion, as if not understanding.

"We want to take you back," I continued my explanation. "But you have to shift into your human form so we can do that—"

Suddenly, a gold mist surrounded her form...and she shifted back.

I had expected more of a fight, but when her body began to drop from the air, I realized that

Bexley had literally passed out. *Shit*. Gage caught her in a snap as I immediately joined him at her side. Lifting my fingers to her pulse, I breathed out a sigh of relief at the steady sound. She must have passed out due to exhaustion—that was the simplest explanation.

My relief was short lived as Jagger gently lifted her golden hair, examining her neck. Ioan's claw marks marred her skin. I closed my eyes momentarily, trying to steady myself from the inferno threatening to burst out from my chest. One that demanded vengeance for my injured mate.

"We can be mad about it later," Jagger bit out. "Let's get her back."

I nodded as we walked towards the front of the cave. Renewed anger welled inside of me because this moment was supposed to be special for Bexley, not some compulsory reaction to a life-or-death situation. More so, if forcibly breaking the spell that locked her memories away had somehow hurt her...

I didn't want to go there. I didn't want to even consider that it had caused even more memory damage. We had always talked about breaking the spell and all the good it could do, but we'd never discussed in detail the possible negative effects it could have on her. We were just eager to get her back.

All I could do right now was pray to the fates that she would be okay.

Deciding I would hold Bexley, Jagger shifted, and I climbed onto his back and secured her against me. The autumn breeze, which had originally felt good, now concerned me. Her clothes were torn and seared from what had occurred in the bathroom, so I was worried she was cold. I wrapped my jacket around her and then Jagger took off, following Gage who was leading the way.

As I examined the perfectly blue skies, I found myself wishing for a storm because I knew it would help her magic. Luckily it was only minutes later that Jagger flew down to land near one of the interconnected bridges of our dorm. I slid off with Bexley in my arms and walked towards her dorm, situated in the center of the structure, feeling relieved that we were back. My gaze moved down to her face as I shifted her, using one hand to open the french doors from her balcony.

Exhaustion was evident in the way she was breathing heavily, having fallen into a deep sleep, but outside of that, the seared clothes, and the already healing mark from Ioan's claws...she looked *okay*. I mean, she was fucking beautiful, from her golden skin to the freckles that covered the bridge of her nose, but I couldn't say she was more than just 'okay' until I watched her open those gold eyes. Until I heard her tell me how she felt.

Then I would consider her more than okay.

Reaching her bed, I pulled back the covers and laid her down, removing her shoes and resting her head on one of the many silk pillows before tucking her in. Moments later, Jagger and Gage joined me, all of us staring down at her. While I felt significantly better that she was in bed resting, my anxiety over her state only grew.

"Everyone saw her shift," Gage murmured.

They had.

"They don't know what type—"

"It will be obvious to some. Very few dragons look like her," I said, countering Jagger's attempt to comfort us. There was no comfort—just the stark truth.

Bexley was a dragon. That wasn't the issue though.

"We just have to do our damn best to protect her," Gage said.

Jagger nodded sharply and turned to the door, calling back, "I'm going to grab a few things she might need." Gage sat in a chair on the side of her bed as I sat on the edge of her mattress, the bed dipping slightly because of my weight.

"News of her shifting into a dragon is going to spread, and fast," I murmured.

"Maybe not." Gage hesitated. "They already assumed she was a female dragon..."

"That's not the part I'm talking about." I offered him a pointed look.

My hand brushed over her face gently, moving a strand of hair out of the way.

No, like I said that wasn't the problem. The true problem?

Bexley wasn't just a dragon—she was a female storm dragon.

Chapter Two

Bexley

"Mom?" I whispered.

My heart was beating a million miles an hour as I stared up at her. She was scared. There was a tremble to her hand as she knocked on the heavy wooden door in front of us once more.

I didn't know where the door led, but the minute the alarms went off, warning us that danger was coming, my mom had taken me from bed and dragged me here. I didn't know where 'here' was though. It was a part of the estate I'd never been to.

"Rebecca!" my mom snarled, her eyes flashing black. "Open this damn door—"

"I heard you," said a shrill voice. A woman pulled open the heavy wooden surface, and I instantly drew back, unable to control my reaction. I had no idea who this woman was, and I would have remembered her if I'd seen her before.

She had one eye, and the half of her face with no eye was covered in green scales—dragon scales. Unlike myself, my mom didn't hesitate, pulling me through the door almost immediately. I looked around, taken off guard by the space we'd entered.

It was beautiful, in a very weird way.

The stone walls were covered with moss, and plants hung in broken lanterns from the ceiling. If it'd been daytime, the light from the windows would have probably made it even prettier. Instead, my gaze was drawn to the cauldron at the center of the room, boiling away on a low simmer.

"We need to do this immediately," my mom demanded. "Surely you heard the alarms."

"What do you think I have been working on?" the woman said patiently and motioned for me to sit. Tears gathered in my mom's eyes, and before I could sit as instructed, she crouched down and gently held my face, looking over my expression. Panic tightened my chest at her sadness, and the words that followed only made it far worse.

"I love you, Bexley," she whispered. "I love you so so much. I have to go away for a little bit, but Rebecca is going to take care of you."

My own tears began to slip down my face because

despite her saying 'a little bit,' it didn't feel like that. It felt like she was being more serious than that. "Don't go, please. Where...where is Dad? Why isn't he here? Wherever you're going, I can come with you. I'll help."

Pain filled her gaze. "Dad is handling a problem—one I have to help him with. I promise that once it's fixed we'll be back, okay?"

I shook my head as a hiccuped sob broke from my throat. No, that wasn't okay. Nothing about this was okay in any way possible. *My breathing was uneven, and I found myself wishing that my friends were here —my brave, strong friends. Gage, Jagger, and Breaker would know what to do. They always knew how to handle things.*

"Remember the stories we told you, about the brave princess? The one that would fight even the scariest creatures?"

I nodded because it was a story they told me often.

"I need you to be brave like that. I need you to be brave for me."

"Okay, Mom," *I whispered as tears fell from her own eyes. Had I ever seen my mom cry before? I couldn't remember, but seeing it right now caused my stomach to drop.*

Mom looked up to Rebecca, giving her a meaningful look before whispering that she loved me and pressing a soft kiss to my forehead. I closed my eyes and clung onto her, unable to handle the idea of her leaving me, but all too soon she was striding towards the door with a determined glint to her expression. I stifled my renewed crying with my hand, realizing that whatever was going on here, I wasn't being the brave princess—she was.

"Alright, little dragon," Rebecca said. "We're going to give you a special drink that's going to make time go by really fast, and then we'll be going to the city. Are you okay with that?"

"Will my parents meet me there?"

"Yes."

Why didn't I believe her? Why did her words ring false? It didn't matter though because my mom trusted Rebecca, and she had told me to be brave. So that was exactly what I would do. Somehow.

"Okay." The woman brought over a small vial and handed it to me, wisps of smoke wafting from the surface. "Down it goes."

I threw the vial back, the liquid scorching my mouth. I whimpered but swallowed it down, the flavor of orange and berry creating an odd sensation on my tongue, almost like it was bubbly in my mouth. But the minute it hit my stomach I began to feel sick, and I closed my eyes as I willed myself not to throw up.

My eyes felt heavy, and I could only briefly hear... what was her name again? I blinked my eyes open and found I couldn't remember her name. Her face, though...I recognized her face. Or did I?

"We'll leave when the spell kicks in fully," she promised me, the warmth in her gaze making me automatically trust her. Or maybe I'd been told to trust her. I couldn't remember.

She continued, "I need you to remember one thing, though. No matter what happens, there is one person you have to avoid. You can't see him."

"Okay," I whispered, but I was confused on where I was, who this lady was, so I wasn't sure about my ability to process any additional information.

Her mouth opened as she said a name. I could hear it, I could even see her saying it, but it didn't stick. I blinked as she said it three more times. On the third, it was accented by the door bursting open. I let out a scream of panic as I was thrown back across the room by a surge of power, Rebecca appearing in front of me defensively.

I could hear snarls and growls, the distinct scent of raw meat filling the space. Rebecca looked at me in abject fear and slammed her hand against my chest, barking out a hard word in a language I didn't recognize.

Everything immediately went dark.

. . .

I flung up in bed, my hand wrapping around my throat as a panicked gasp got caught there. My eyes were wide open, and I was staring into the darkness of a bedroom. That was all I could focus on besides my body's reaction to the dream I'd just had.

My temples were pulsating in pain, and tears were hot on my cheeks. I was shaking as emotions ran wild within me, ranging from fury to heartache. I didn't understand any of it though. I didn't understand why that dream had evoked such a reaction from me. Unless...

Well, unless it hadn't been a dream and was instead a memory.

Letting out a shaky breath, trying to calm my pulse, that idea rang true to me. Was that what it had been? A memory? Of when? How old had I been? Was that truly my mom?

Fresh tears welled in my eyes as I pulled my knees up against my body and tried to ignore the sickening sensation in my gut that told me that something very, very bad had happened that night. More than the memory even showcased.

Falling back against my pillow, I tried to pull out of the haze of my dream and instead focus on my reality.

I was in my bedroom in the dorm.

I was lying curled up on my massive circular bed that was made of pale pink and gold bedding. The deep blue sky above me, visible from the windows that curved up the back wall and along the ceiling, told me it was evening. But how had I gotten here? And how long had I been asleep?

Closing my eyes, I ran through what I could last remember. Almost instantly the memory surfaced, making my gut churn.

Ioan. He'd cornered me. Not only cornered me but threatened me...tried to kill me. My breath caught as the full memory began to filter in. *He actually tried to kill me.* And then something happened. Everything around me had exploded into a fiery inferno, and my skin felt like it had burst from the seams—

"I shifted." I flung up in bed and looked down at my skin. My clothes were seared but intact, and my hands seemed to almost shimmer with gold flecks embedded in my skin, but otherwise I looked the same. I didn't *feel* the same, though.

I shifted. In the center of my being, a fire had roared to life, proving my instincts right. I had finally shifted...but into what?

It didn't hurt to think about, but I was met with a fuzzy wall of confusion regarding the past few hours of my life. I closed my eyes and tried to pull on the energy inside of me, trying to recognize what I was and feeling eager to test it out, but my magic resisted. Apparently it was absolutely drained.

Okay...so not yet then.

"Gage? Jagger? Breaker?" I called, opening my eyes and seeking them out in the room. I needed to talk to one of my mates.

My mates. I inhaled, realizing that my temples didn't hurt from the thought at all—not even in the slightest—as they had before. In fact, even thinking back along the line of questions that usually caused pain, I was met with no physical warnings of the agony to come. Instead there was just a foggy haze, like when the mirror steamed up after a hot shower. Already it was starting to clear, the edges of my memory barely revealing themselves, but enough so I knew something had changed.

I had a feeling it would eventually reveal the truth. All of it. I just had no idea what to expect from that truth.

When no one responded to my call, I slipped from my bed and winced. My limbs felt tight and my muscles sore, but outside of that, I felt good. Really good, in fact. I reached my hands above my head and inhaled deeply, then exhaled. I ran my hand over my neck, expecting soreness there because I keenly remembered the bite of Ioan's claws, but instead found nothing.

What had happened to Ioan? I felt dread at the idea of seeing him again, and I knew how my mates would react to what he did. I was kind of looking forward to it. I shouldn't have thought like that, but there was a darkness in my head that told me he would deserve whatever pain they served him, that as my mates they should do that...

No. That was wrong...right? I shook my head and focused on finding my men so they could tell me what had happened.

Why was I back in the dorm? How had I gotten back? What had I shifted into? How long had I been shifted? All the unknowns left me with a feeling of uneasiness.

Before leaving my bedroom, I quickly slipped off my seared clothes and pulled on a pair of velvet joggers and a matching sweater in pale pink. It was one of my most comfortable sets, and right now, I needed comfort, and a lot of it.

Although I would have preferred it in the form of my mates.

Leaving my lantern-lit room, I stepped into the main space of my dorm and frowned at finding it empty. I didn't like that at all. Despite trying to push the intrusive thoughts from my head, I couldn't help but wonder why they weren't here. Sure, I may not have known Jagger and Breaker as well as Gage—

I stopped on that thought because suddenly it didn't ring as true as before. In my memory/dream, I had thought about the three of them...but I was coming up blank on why that would be. I had to assume we'd been friends though.

Either way, I knew without a doubt that Gage would never leave me alone after what had happened today, and I didn't think the other two would stand for that either.

Unless...I had made it back here myself and they didn't even know what happened?

My magic rose in my chest as I froze, the unfamiliar sensation both exhilarating and a bit scary, causing me to inhale sharply and bring a hand to my chest. Almost like forcing a memory on me, a scene flashed through my head. Flying through the sky, arcing around in a circle and catching sight of three massive forms behind me.

Dragons. I had been flying with dragons. *Their* dragons. My mates.

Wait—I could fly? Holy crap, I could fly!

That truth resonated inside of me, and I swayed slightly on my toes, a smile growing on my face. I wanted to know so badly what I'd turned into. Whatever it was, I was thrilled. After all, I could fly with my mates now. Maybe an owl? An eagle? Some other type of bird? As much as I loved the small snippets of memories, they weren't telling me nearly as much as I needed.

"Breaker? Jagger? Gage?" I called out again, louder this time. "Guys?"

Looking around the space, I saw a dark figure walking along one of the distant bridges and immediately made my way towards the french doors. As I opened the glass entrance, his head snapped over and I nearly melted in relief.

Gage Bronzeheart.

In a second flat, he was in front of me, and I didn't hesitate to wrap my arms around him and bury my head against his massive chest. His large hand dug into my hair as he pressed me further against him, and a deep rumble came from his chest. One that felt instantly familiar and lit up a part of me that I was now recognizing came from my... animal? My shifted counterpart?

That was going to take some getting used to. Where before my animal had been silent, covered up in layers upon layers of stifling magic, it was now brilliant and bold. Despite not knowing its identity, I felt it there, right under my skin.

"Fuck, Bex, I was so damn worried. I'm sorry I wasn't in there when you woke up. I was trying to get some fresh air and get my head on straight. The other two went to grab some other things you may need," he whispered. "We had no idea how you would feel waking up."

I pulled back and stared up into his gorgeous green eyes, concerned about the uncharacteristic rambling and the sight of a frazzled Gage. The man was unfairly gorgeous, even in this moment—maybe *especially* in this moment. The sight of him unraveling appealed to a part of me I didn't fully understand.

His emerald eyes were dark, swirling with bronze streaks that I knew belonged to his dragon... but suddenly that concept didn't feel exactly right. I had always known it was a sign of his dragon, but after feeling the vibrant flame inside of myself, it was crystal clear that it wasn't a completely separate entity, but rather a part of himself.

So all those times he had blamed stuff on his dragon... Oh fates, he really did like me. And not just because of some mating connection kicking in. Things were starting to make a lot more sense now, but I had more pressing questions, so I would hold off on confirming my theory.

I offered him a small smile and asked softly, "Because I shifted, right? It was because I shifted that you guys were worried."

Relief, most likely at me remembering what happened, filled Gage's gaze as he nodded once. "Yeah, cupcake, you shifted."

Emotion crowded my throat, making me feel momentarily overwhelmed. This was such a big moment, and while I wished Ioan hadn't been the catalyst, I wasn't going to let that ruin it.

I had shifted. I had *finally* shifted!

"What did I shift into?" I asked curiously, trying to move his mind away from the possibility that I was injured. I felt great, but I knew that voicing that wouldn't make Gage feel better—the man was constantly hyper-focused on my safety.

His eyes widened just slightly in surprise. "You don't remember?"

"My memory is a bit fuzzy. I know what happened with—"

"Don't say his name," Gage nearly begged, tension running through his frame as he closed his eyes, his grip tightening on me. "Don't say his name right now. I've been on the edge of hunting him down since we got back here."

I smoothed a hand over his chest in understanding. "I remember that part, and then I remember being in the air with you three, but nothing else," I whispered before adding, "It doesn't hurt, though, to think about it. To think about anything, really... It feels like something has changed. I have to tell you guys about this dream—"

Gage's lips interrupted me, molding to mine in an excited kiss that left me breathless. It was filled with so much intensity and happiness that when he pulled back I wasn't surprised to see so much hope and light in his gaze. "It doesn't hurt to think about? At all? What about the memories that used to cause you pain?"

"Nothing." I couldn't help but smile back at him before explaining, "Things are a bit hazy, but no pain."

"Thank the fates," he rumbled, pressing his forehead to mine. "I'm sure things will slowly come back to you, but I can't handle the idea of you being in pain."

"Gage." I tilted my head back and examined his face. "What did I shift into?" It was driving me crazy not knowing.

His eyes filled with warmth. A bit of concern as well, but I wasn't sure at what. "A dragon, Bex. You shifted into a dragon."

For a prolonged moment, silence filled the air as I stared at him in shock, not fully comprehending the words that he'd just said. Pure, unadulterated joy slammed into me as tears of happiness welled in my eyes. The flame in the center of my chest roared brightly, and obsidian strings unraveled from the flame and reached out to him, vibrating with truth.

A dragon. I was a dragon? How often had I prayed to the fates for that?

"I hope those are happy tears," Gage murmured, picking me up under my butt and lifting me to eye level.

"Of course they are." I gave him a watery smile, putting my hands on either side of his face and trying to infuse as much emotion as possible in my voice. "How could they not be?"

"I can't wait to see your reaction to what you look like shifted," he said. "You are glorious. Absolute perfection."

The door to the elevator opened, and I turned my head, unable to stop smiling as my other mates entered through my dorm.

Instantly, I caught both Breaker and Jagger's confused, panicked, and concerned expressions—probably because of the tears.

"You're back!" I slid down Gage's frame, who allowed me a bit of room from him but not much. It was hard to put space between him and me, even if I wanted to, because his grip was unyielding, and considering he was 6'6" and stacked with muscles... If he didn't want me to move, I wasn't moving.

Why did I love that so much?

"Is everything okay?" Jagger demanded, his eyes darkening as he tossed down the bags on the island. "Fuck. You're crying."

"Happiness," I promised. "I'm crying because I'm happy."

Realization shone in his gaze. "You remember. You remember what happened? About shifting?"

"Are you injured? Sore?" Breaker asked before I could answer, adding his bags to the mix as I nodded in response to Jagger's first question. "Yes, I remember, at least mostly...and I feel great," I explained and then stepped back inside through the french doors, Gage loosening his grip. "We have so much we need to talk about." I paused, looking up at Gage. "*That dream.* I have to tell you guys about it."

"What dream?" Jagger asked as he approached, crossing the cozy space towards me.

"It was a dream about my mom... And the night I lost my memory."

Chapter Three

Bexley

"Okay, explain that dream," Jagger suggested softly.

It had been around thirty minutes since I'd dropped the not-so-small bomb that I'd dreamed about the night that I'd lost...well, everything. At least I'd thought I lost everything—my family, my life, my memories—but instead they'd been tucked away, waiting for me to rediscover them. And while I didn't have all of them right now, I suspected Gage was right—they would come back.

"We should wait for Breaker." I pointed to my dorm's small modern kitchen, where he was preparing something for me. I knew Jagger and Gage were impatient considering the circumstances, not just with the memory but everything that had happened today, but I wanted all my mates around me when I told the story. It wasn't exactly the easiest dream to explain, but unlike most dreams it didn't seem to be going anywhere. The details were right at the front of my mind and easy to retrieve.

A lost memory now found.

Plus, I was enjoying looking at my mates, especially since we were all in the same space together. I knew once I began recounting the dream I would be far too distracted to appreciate that fact.

Gage was pacing behind the couch in thought, his gaze moving between me and the roaring fireplace, and Jagger was sitting on the cream-colored velvet couch right across from where I was curled up in a chair with a cozy blanket around me.

"Alright." Jagger nodded in understanding, standing up and pressing a kiss to the top of my head before going to help Breaker in the kitchen, probably to expedite the process.

It still surprised me just how beautiful and luxurious these dorms were. Not that I wasn't used to luxury—the Bronzeheart estate had been something out of a dream. My dream, specifically, as in tailored to anything I had wanted... And this dorm very much followed suit.

The living area was currently bathed in shadows from the night sky, which was visible from the back wall of windows that, much like my bedroom, arched up into the roof in a greenhouse effect. The balcony doors were currently open, allowing for the cool night wind to brush through, making me eager to walk outside.

It was such a unique dorm setup, with each of the four dorms featuring a wrap-around balcony. The guys' three dorms were connected by bridges on the perimeter, and another set of bridges connected each of their dorms to mine in the center. It was the perfect setup for the four of us, and I once again couldn't escape the feeling that it had been very purposeful.

If it was, I would love it all the more.

"Cupcake." Gage appeared in front of me, crouching to be eye level with me. "What are you thinking about?"

"Just how much I love the dorm," I admitted easily.

Warmth infused his gaze. "Good. That was the idea."

My smile grew because I was even more sure of my theory now. "Why? Did you want me to like it?" I teased.

"Yes, little treasure. In fact, I wish you were in it way more often as it is," Jagger said as he returned with a cup of hot tea. I took it gratefully, the smell of peppermint from the tea mixing with Jagger's very similar scent. The man was so intoxicating to be around that sometimes I found myself distracted, the combustible reaction he elicited in my body leaving me a bit out of breath.

Tonight his silver hair, streaked with black, was a bit messier than normal, most likely from running his hand through it, and his lean-cut, corded muscles were covered in a dark shirt that contrasted his icy skin. He was so large—they all were—that it made the dorm feel that much more cozy despite him having a naturally icy gaze that would unnerve most. My eyes moved to the rune on the left side of his jaw and the earring there, and not for the first time I found myself wanting to run my fingers along the tattoo and ask him about it.

I knew he would let me.

Despite being a confusing mixture of both having all the control in the world and none at all, Jagger had made it clear how he felt about me.

Finally processing his words, I offered a small scowl. "I may love it, but I also love school. I can't stay inside all the time—I would go crazy!"

Unless I was with them, of course.

"Then maybe the rest of the students should leave," Jagger grumbled, causing Gage to chuckle. He then tacked on, "Just the male students would do

—I know you have your female friend, little treasure."

The flame inside of me sparked at his possessive words about the males, and I also loved that he wanted to make sure I still had Rachel by my side. Although he probably needed to learn her name at some point...

"Wait." I frowned in realization. "Then it would be just you three and a bunch of girls—I don't like that either." It was nothing against the other girls, I just knew how hard it was to *not* look at my mates, and I was finding I was more than a little possessive over them.

"Possessive. I love it." Gage kissed my forehead and stood up, probably going to take a seat. Before I could respond to his accurate comment, Breaker walked around the couch with a bowl in his hand.

"The rest of you grab some too," he ordered roughly, his voice causing a smile to tug at my lips. There was something about his gruff voice—heck, something about Breaker in general—that really drew me in. It was probably why I'd sought him out that first night I stayed in the dorms before even 'meeting him' officially. Somehow I'd known without a doubt that I could trust him.

I'm sure part of it was because of our past, a touch of the locked-away memories breaking through my subconscious, but once I was around him it was clear that my instincts were imploring me to trust him. It was that simple.

Once the others had grabbed their bowls, my tea sitting nearby on the coffee table, I began to eat the pasta carbonara he'd made, trying to determine the best way to describe the dream. I wanted to make sure I relayed everything accurately, especially since they may be able to fill in some of the blanks for me.

And there were a lot of blanks. I had so many questions, and I'm sure my mates did too. I was thanking the fates for the lack of pain associated with thinking about all of it now.

The fear had left a mark on me though. I could feel myself instinctually preparing for pain whenever I went to think about anything related to my past, only to be met by relief. It would probably take a bit to get used to that.

"Thank you, this is delicious," I said to Breaker.

The impossibly massive man graced me with a smile that I knew he didn't offer many. I swear, the dragon looked like a warrior out of some fantasy novel. From his messy blond hair that was currently pushed back, to the scar on his jaw that was multiplied on his chest, the man exuded this rough power that was so appealing to me. Then there were his unique eyes, one so dark it was nearly black and the other gold, because of his dragon. I had no idea if it was because of his magic or if he was born with such a stunning contrast, but I could have easily stared at them all day.

"Never a problem, *mo chuisle.*"

"Alright." Gage sat down, and Jagger joined him. "We're all here. Ready to listen."

"Let her eat."

"It's fine," I promised Breaker, taking a bite of my pasta. "I can do both. I eat a lot, so if I couldn't talk during meals, I wouldn't get much done —ever."

Jagger offered me a curious look, and I shrugged because it was an accurate statement.

"She's not wrong," Gage agreed.

Deciding to jump right into it, I took another bite and closed my eyes, relaying all the details of the dream to them from the fear in my mother's eyes as we knocked on Rebecca's door, to our tearful good-bye, to Rebecca making me drink something before the door crashed in. They listened the entire time, and I was hoping they'd be able to give even more perspective on it.

Concluding the story, I raised a question. "We were being attacked, right? The alarms were going off, and my mom seemed scared."

"And you don't remember the name Rebecca

told you?" Jagger asked, his gaze hyper-focused on me, not answering my question right away.

I shook my head, disappointed. "I imagine I'll remember eventually, but that's all I've got."

"Someone did attack you," Gage confirmed, "and the inability to pin down who led the attack has caused a divide for eight years now."

"What?" My eyes widened in confusion. "What do you mean?"

"You should tell her everything," Breaker suggested, and I nodded in agreement. Now that we didn't have to worry about it causing me pain, I wanted to know it all. I wanted to understand.

Gage stood in front of the fireplace as I put down my pasta bowl, a dissatisfied sound coming from Breaker. "If at any point this hurts—"

"It won't," I promised. "But I'll tell you if it does."

"You've known all of us since you were about six," Gage started. My brows shot up. I knew I'd come to the Bronzeheart estate at ten, so to say that was surprising... Well, actually it wasn't. Something about that felt right. Though I didn't understand how someone like me would have come to know them... Had my family been ruled by one of their clans? Or maybe worked for their parents?

"We met at a function at your family's estate," Gage continued.

"Wait..." I frowned. "The three clans were at my family's house? Why?"

"I promise we'll get to that," Gage said with a look of understanding. I sat back, silently promising I wouldn't ask any more questions till he told me everything.

"So we met when you were six, and for the next four years, we were inseparable. If you weren't at one of our houses, then we were at yours. We were even tutored together," he explained. My lips pressed up, loving the sound of that. "Then everything changed right after your tenth birthday.

"Your family was attacked one night. No one knows who did it because the only evidence left was the carnage—"

"Gage!" Breaker growled. Gage winced, and I bit my lip, trying not to think too much about the idea of my family...

Nope. Not going there.

"Keep going," I encouraged, removing that detail from my thoughts.

"No one knows who attacked your family, and everyone thought that you'd been lost as well. Clearly we know differently now, and when we found you without your memories in that alleyway, it was clear something horrible had happened.

"Remember when I said the clans don't trust one another anymore? That's because of the mistrust of that night, because no one knows who led the attack on your family, which is why my family kept your identity quiet. Even their parents don't know you are alive," Gage continued as Jagger nodded. "Although, I would have to assume they suspect something."

"Never said anything to me, but yeah, I think they know something is up," Breaker said, looking frustrated.

"So because of that, Jagger and Breaker couldn't officially come to see you. Plus, whenever we even mentioned the other heirs, you'd get horrible headaches, so we were worried what being physically around them would do," Gage explained.

"Okay, that's...that's horrible," I swallowed. "So the clans don't trust each other because you think it's possible that one of your families killed mine?"

"The three of us don't think that." Jagger shook his head. "And I think the other clans may have realized it was a bad assumption as well, but considering we still don't know who attacked your family, it leaves room for suspicion."

"So if I had more context for my dream, it would help a ton," I murmured.

"Essentially," Gage agreed.

"Okay...but why? Why would someone attack my family? Why did we even know one another?"

Breaker made a low sound in his throat as they exchanged looks.

Finally, Gage crouched down in front of me and took my hand. "Because, Bexley, you're an heir as well."

* * *

"What?!" I stared at him in shock, unable to process his words.

"It's true. Your family ruled the Flash Clan—"

"No." I shook my head, interrupting him. "Listen, I can understand shifting into a dragon. I mean, I'm still shocked by that, but at least I can rationalize it. But now you're saying that my parents ruled a dragon clan and that I'm an heir? That's impossible. One of my parents would have to be—"

"A storm dragon," Gage said, his expression filled with understanding. "And *you* are a storm dragon as well."

I blinked and stood up, walking around the armchair to shake myself, not taking full stock in his words.

Nope, there was no way he meant what he said.

A storm dragon? That was impossible. It was one thing to be a dragon, but a *storm* dragon?

"So you're saying my parents were clan leaders and I'm...I'm an heir? A storm dragon heir? A female storm dragon?"

"Yes," Jagger rumbled.

"This is not good," I whispered, looking down at the floor. I'd heard about female storm dragons and everything they'd been put through in history, and none of it was good. Literally none of it.

It didn't help that there were other thoughts running through my brain. Part of it was telling me to feel grief for the loss of my parents, but because I had no memories associated with them, I just felt clogged up. Like I wasn't reacting correctly.

"Everything is going to be fine." Breaker appeared in front of me, pulling me against him. "Seriously, Bexley, everything—"

"But it won't," I said, turning my head against his chest to look at Gage. "Someone was clearly after my family, and once they realize I'm still alive—"

"Nothing will happen," Gage growled in denial, but it didn't soothe my concern.

"We would never let anyone hurt you," Jagger promised, his eyes shading with darkness. "The thing with Ioan today will never happen again."

Ioan. Fates. I'd completely forgotten about him.

My eyes went wide as I broke from Breaker and sat on the edge of the chair, running a hand over my face. "I didn't even ask—what happened to him? And everyone saw me shift, didn't they? I mean, I broke through the roof, right?" Suddenly my happiness and pure joy at not only shifting but being told I was a dragon was turning into panic.

"They saw you shift," Breaker confirmed, "but they just know you're a dragon, something they already suspected. They wouldn't know you're a storm dragon. They don't know the signs, and it was a clear day out, so the magic you would normally pull from storms wasn't present."

"We just have to be careful with that until we can identify who went after your family and determine if they have any descendants here...assuming that it wasn't one of our clans," Jagger said.

I let out a shaky breath and drew in my bottom lip. "I've *got* to remember that name. That would help, right?" This was so damn frustrating. I knew my mom had Rebecca remove my memories for a reason, but I didn't fully understand why. Wouldn't it make more sense for me to know who to avoid? Then again, Rebecca had clearly tried to tell me *after* the memory spell, it just hadn't worked.

"And we need you to avoid shifting unless we're in private. As it is, we don't shift a lot on campus,"

Jagger said. I nodded in understanding, taking a deep breath to calm myself down.

"Okay," I said softly, my brows furrowing. "So just...act normal?" I wasn't all that great at that to begin with.

"As normal as people will let us act," Breaker rumbled. "Now that they know you're a dragon, it'll change things, even if they'd already assumed you would eventually turn into a dragon."

"Okay, I'll try," I said, though I was already nervous at the thought of interacting with anyone else. "At least we don't have classes until Monday. Maybe that will allow everything to cool off a bit."

"Hopefully. Plus, tonight is the Black Moon, so we're staying in anyway," Gage said. "I already locked all the doors to the other dorms. We're going to sleep in here, cupcake—don't want any shifter bastards breaking in here."

I shivered in revulsion, thinking about what happened with Ioan.

"So do we want to watch a movie or something?" I suggested, not knowing what else to do. I mean, what I'd just found out...that wasn't something you processed in minutes. I needed to sleep on it, and more so, I needed to let my thoughts settle because right now they were moving a million miles an hour.

"After you eat," Breaker rumbled. I sat back

down and speared a piece of pasta with my fork, a hesitant smile pulling at my lips. I may have felt nervous, but around my mates, I knew I was safe.

It didn't escape my notice that they didn't answer my question about Ioan and how he was doing, though. Maybe it was better I didn't know.

Chapter Four

Bexley

It wasn't until the next morning, while sipping on morning coffee after waking up somewhat late, that I realized my night of sleep had been completely dreamless. I'd slept straight through the night with a heavy sense of comfort and safety that came from my mates. My mates, who had insisted on taking shifts staying up to make sure no other shifters bothered our dorms...and who were far more tired than I was right now.

Before I'd experienced the manic and irrational fury that had come off of Ioan when he attacked me, I would've thought it was unneeded to be that concerned, but now I wasn't sure. Ioan was not a nice guy, I had easily recognized that from the start in how he treated those around him, but the more I thought about it—panic tightening my throat whenever I did—the more I realized that in that bathroom he had been something else entirely.

Something completely monstrous and terrifying.

"Wow," I whispered as Gage walked through the door and offered me a reckless, charming smile. One that was far more relaxed and more 'him' then I'd seen since arriving. I loved it, but that wasn't why I was saying 'wow.'

Maybe I should have mediated my reaction with my other mate sitting right next to me on the couch, but Breaker just chuckled as I looked over Gage's uniform, which had caused my initial reaction. Dark athletic pants and a jersey that was tight against his muscular torso. I'd never seen him dressed in a uniform like this, and it honestly left me a bit breathless.

"Thanks, cupcake." Gage winked, causing my cheeks to flush. I had never been one to worry about or try to control my reactions, but since discovering I was mates with these men, my emotions growing far more complicated, I was finding the habit could be a bit embarrassing at times.

"You have a game today," I said, stating the obvious. Jagger made a concerned noise in his throat as he made a cup of coffee, probably because he knew where I was going with this. While the three of us had stayed in pajamas, relaxing on the late Saturday morning, I should've realized something was up when Gage disappeared.

"I do," he said, ducking his head as he slid on a pair of shoes. What I *thought* I saw in his eyes before he looked down was sadness, but why would he be...

"I'm going," I said immediately while standing up. Gage snapped his head up, and his eyes filled with a warm light, though it was tinged with concern. I was going to guess that he wanted me to go but didn't think it was a good idea or something along those lines.

I was totally still going.

Breaker dragged me down to his lap, making a low rumble as my eyes widened, realizing just how hard he was. Luckily, Jagger's next words brought me back to the present, keeping me from turning around and kissing Breaker... Or maybe that was unlucky.

"I'm not sure that's a good idea, little treasure. People will be talking about what happened yesterday, which will put you right at the center of attention." Something I knew Jagger hated, and while I used to think it came from a place of embarrassment, I was now realizing it was something far different than that.

Jagger was being protective.

"Let them talk," I said dismissively. "Like you said, half of them already assumed I'm a dragon.

Plus, I'm not missing Gage's game—the first game of the year, at that!"

"We do have a separate seating area, so it would be fairly safe," Gage murmured, causing me to smile. *He totally wanted me to go.*

I shimmied on Breaker's lap, causing him to groan before releasing me, and walked towards Gage. I looped my arms around him, and he dipped his head so we were closer.

"I'm excited to see you play," I admitted before tilting my head in realization that I'd never been to a sporting event before, at least not one like this. "What do I wear?"

"My jersey," Gage answered immediately, Jagger letting out a low, amused sound.

"Okay." I nodded eagerly, loving the sound of that. "You get me the jersey, and I promise we will be there watching you."

"Thanks, cupcake." Gage pressed a fleeting kiss to my lips before disappearing, leaving me stunned in the best way possible. When he appeared seconds later with a gold and black jersey for me, his name proudly on the back, I took it greedily. He didn't realize it yet, but he was *never* getting this back.

"Good luck." I rolled up on my toes and kissed him again before he left, leaving me with the other two.

"You have no idea how happy you just made him," Jagger said as he appeared behind me. I smiled up at him, because I was almost positive I did. Or at least a little bit.

"I hope so. I'm excited to go," I admitted as Breaker said something about our seats, allowing me to escape to the bathroom as Jagger turned to answer him. I knew they would have to get ready as well, so I tried to get showered and dressed quickly, not wanting to miss any of the game.

After I was wrapped in a robe, I brushed out the curls I'd created before adding some light makeup. When I was done, I slipped out of the room and went to my bedroom, grabbing a pair of sparkly black jeans and long-sleeve turtleneck to go with the jersey. I could tell it was a bit chilly outside, so I paired the entire outfit with a pair of gold bottom high heel boots and a gold and black scarf I'd knitted a year or so back.

Turning in the mirror, I let out a pleased sound at how I looked, deciding at the last minute to tie up the oversized jersey to show off my high-waisted jeans. *Perfection*.

"Little treasure—*shit*," Jagger groaned. I turned to look at him, noticing that he was wearing dark jeans and a long-sleeve shirt that featured the academy's name. *Dark Imaginarium Academy*. The crest was prominent, paired with the shifter sector's colors. *How the heck did I get a shirt like that?*

"What?" I asked curiously.

"You look perfect," Breaker said. He'd appeared behind Jagger, dressed similarly. "Ignore him, he's just being possessive."

"Over what?" *I loved the idea of Jagger being possessive over me, so I was all ears.*

The man in question was still staring at me, almost as if he was in pain. "Male shifters seeing you look so good," he rumbled, tugging my hand so that I was brought against his chest. "You are so damn appealing, little treasure, to literally fucking everyone."

"I doubt that," I murmured, flushing at the compliment. I didn't really think I held as much appeal as he was saying, but if he wanted to think I was that attractive...well, I wouldn't freakin' complain.

"Right," he grumbled, shaking his head. "Come on, let's go."

As we went down the elevator, me captured between the two of them, I began to feel that trickle of nerves roll over me once again. Mostly because they were right that there'd be a lot of eyes on me. I normally wouldn't care about people looking at me—it seemed to be a common occurrence when it came to the men I surrounded myself with—but right now it was because of a situation I wasn't equipped to handle.

Almost as if knowing, Breaker spoke softly. "We don't have to go. Gage will understand."

"I want to go, I'm just not sure how people will react."

"Fear and respect, most likely," Jagger said. "That's how they treat most dragons."

But I wasn't most dragons, and I couldn't imagine someone fearing me. "I don't want anyone to fear me."

"It's instinctual," Breaker explained, his voice filled with understanding. "The aura your magic gives off is significantly different now that the spell has broken. Less dominant shifters won't be able to help but fear you. Of course your personality will play a part and most likely soften the effect, but at the end of the day, you're a dragon."

I'm a dragon. *Insane.*

"But like we said," he went on, "we have a separate seating area, so don't think too much about it. I promise it'll be fine."

I hoped he was right.

As we made our way across the chilled campus, I noticed large groups of students heading towards the practice field where everything had happened with

Gage. Where he had nearly attacked Fletcher, kissed me, and told me I was his mate. It was the moment where everything had started to click together, when I'd started to fight for the memories despite the pain.

I almost tripped as I remembered what Fletcher had said that made me pass out. *"Because you're a dragon."* He'd told me that. He'd known. But he hadn't feared me...so maybe others wouldn't either. Maybe I could fight that and make sure people were comfortable with me.

As we neared the entrance, that hope was squashed as I began to see what the boys had been talking about. Before, people had been offering me odd looks filled with confusion and fear when it came to my interaction with my mates, but now they were averting their eyes from me. I saw anger there also, which I didn't understand, but it was enough to make me nervous.

Breaker's hand on my back tightened, and Jagger shook his head in frustration. My expression was apparently making it very clear that I was, in fact, noticing everyone's reactions to me.

"Ignore them," Jagger said quietly.

I nodded but couldn't follow the direction because my eyes darted everywhere. Luckily, I didn't see anyone I recognized. I think that would've hurt far more, if someone that I knew, like Rachel, started to avoid me.

As we entered the stadium, I looked for Gage on the field. Both teams seemed to be shifters, but they had jerseys that heavily featured opposite colors of the shifter sector. Gage's team had black with accents of gold, and the other the opposite.

How did they split teams here? Maybe from different years? That didn't seem like it'd be fair, though—wouldn't the seniors be far stronger than the freshmen? I would have to ask.

Climbing up the stairs, I managed to get a better view of the stadium and perked up as I saw Gage. He waved to me, a smile on his face, and people around us began whispering and shooting furtive glances in my direction. Breaker and Jagger led me to a box at the top of the stadium, and as we entered the room from a door on the side, I was happy to see that it was a rather cozy space. It featured comfortable seating, food, beverages, and heating. I wasn't positive why my mates got to sit up here—I had to assume it was something to do with shifter hierarchy—but I wouldn't complain.

Curious, I started to ask, but before I could the game started, and after that my attention was on the field. I peppered the guys with questions, only breaking to cheer for Gage. I learned that there were four teams led by senior captains. The teams were formed not by year, but rather by the type of shifter.

The violence on the field made it necessary to have some level of equality in skill, and every time someone hit another person or blood was spilled in a collision, I couldn't help but wince. If Gage hadn't been so lethal and large I would've worried about him, but he absolutely dominated the field.

I was so entertained by the game that I didn't even realize it was halftime until people were standing and stretching.

"Ten minutes until it starts back up," Jagger explained.

"Just enough time to talk," a feminine voice said from the row of seats beneath us, a girl walking up to position herself in front of me. I instantly recognized her as the girl from the dining hall that Jagger had referred to as a viper.

Diane, was it?

I didn't get a good feeling from Diane, but I didn't exactly get a bad one either. My gaze moved to the people around her, and I realized that the 'bad' energy was coming from them, so I kept my attention on her. She was looking effortlessly as perfect as the first time we'd met, wearing a simple hoodie and watching me with a curious and clinical expression.

I didn't think Diane knew what to make of me. To be fair, the feeling was mutual.

"Leave. Now." Breaker demanded, appearing next to me. Jagger was on my other side, shaking his head in frustration.

I squeezed Breaker's hand in comfort as I offered Diane a curious look. "What do you want to talk about?" My hope was that if I kept it a lighthearted conversation, this weird animosity would go away. I had no reason to dislike her, and I hoped she had no reason to dislike me.

"We want to know what you did to Ioan," one of the men behind her spit out.

Diane silenced him with a snarl before slowly looking back at me, her gaze filled with caution and distrust. "That's exactly what we want to know," she stated evenly. "We know he sustained enough burns to kill him and that you shifted at the same time. I'm not going to assume that it was an accident, so what happened?"

Was...was Ioan dead? She didn't say he was dead, just that he had enough burns to kill him. The guys would've told me if he was dead, right? Holy fates.

Jagger let out a dangerous rumble that had me curling my toes. I loved that sound, and in this moment, it did a lot to calm me down. "She does not answer to you—she answers to nobody."

Diane paled as she looked back at me, keeping her chin tilted up. "I'd like to hear her say that, then."

I didn't have an answer to that. *Did I answer to anyone?* I answered to those that I loved and cared about, but that was because of those relationships. I suppose in this context I didn't...

Deciding to not answer that, I eased past it. "To answer your first question, I was using the bathroom. Ioan cornered me and tried to choke me, accused me of using my body to keep my mates around—" A weird flash of a memory came over me, allowing her to interrupt.

"So they are your mates, and you're a dragon!" she demanded, although she was hardly asking.

"Yes," I confirmed, moving on before she could ask questions that I couldn't answer about my shifted side. "Ioan choked me, and I shifted. That's what happened."

I should've felt guilty about him being burned and injured in the crossfire, but every time I went to feel that way, I thought about how panicked and scared I'd been. How I'd thought I was going to die.

Diane examined my face before exhaling in frustration. "She's telling the truth, I can tell."

Her group seemed to be dissatisfied with that, so I added, "I have no reason to lie."

"You're happy he's hurt," another girl accused.

"I'm not happy he's hurt." I tilted my chin up. "I'm happy he's not around. I don't want to see him again; it's that simple."

At least I hoped it was.

"You won't," Breaker promised. I loved that the two of them were bookends to me, keeping me insulated in their affection while letting me handle this.

Diane's eyes darted away for a moment before returning back to me. "Just stay away from him from now on."

Somehow it felt more of a warning and less of a command, and for sure not because she was mad at me. There was sadness and disappointment in her gaze. I didn't understand it fully, but it made me feel empathy for her. It was almost like she felt responsible for Ioan's actions.

I nodded, and when they left I slumped against Jagger. I noticed other students were staring at me with a bit less aggression than before, although I didn't know why—maybe because they'd overheard what Ioan did? Was that...was that why they were mad at me? Did they think I'd hurt Ioan just for kicks?

With that thought, I felt a bit more somber

watching the rest of the game, my attention straying randomly in thought. Jagger and Breaker were talking, but my gaze kept moving to Diane, feeling like there was a lot more to her story than I understood.

"She's an alpha, but that isn't a power signature that you would recognize, because you're a dragon. Unless it's an alpha that's more powerful than you, it feels like everyone else, until you learn what to look for," Breaker explained, clearly catching where my attention was drifting. "She's one of the students that has taken many of the miscellaneous shifters, not living under clan rule or from the city, under her wing. Kids who don't have alliances with anyone."

"The academy can be a scary place when you have no one," Jagger said. I believed that, and I was beyond thankful that I had my mates. I had thought I would only have Gage here, but I had so much more than that.

I had an entire past to discover.

Suddenly a knock on the door had Breaker turning around and crossing the room. When he opened it up and I saw security there, dread formed in my stomach. This couldn't be good.

"What?" Breaker demanded.

"Professor Clanguard would like to speak to Ms. Bronzeheart as well as all three dragon heirs," the security guard said quietly. Judging by the whispers in the stands, though, everyone below had heard him.

"We'll go to his office after the game then," Breaker bit out, shooting a look to the man in question, who was coaching on the sideline.

"His house on campus," the security guard amended.

"Fine."

When the door closed and Breaker came back over, I felt my stomach drop. Gage scored a try—the rugby version of a touchdown, the guys had taught me—but I could barely focus on that. Why did I have a feeling Professor Clanguard wanted to see me about Ioan? I couldn't think of any other reason than him.

"Everything will be fine," Jagger murmured.

I hoped he was right.

Chapter Five

Gage Bronzeheart

The horns announcing the game's completion sounded loudly through the stadium. I was over the railing and into the rows of seating in a second flat, sprinting up the stairs towards my mate. I heard Coach Clanguard call out my name, but I barely heard it, everything completely overshadowed by the uncertainty and trepidation I could see on Bex's face.

It was clear her thoughts were a million miles away, only half-heartedly reacting to the cheers around her before she joined in, standing and searching for me on the field. She didn't realize I was already on my way towards her. I could tell the visit from security had rocked her, and I needed to know what they'd said to make her look so anxious.

I was already furious at them, but if the look on

Jagger and Breaker's faces were anything to go by, I had a feeling there was much more to be mad about than I realized.

Security had no damn reason to be approaching my cupcake. I knew they understood the rules here—the spoken and unspoken hierarchy—and I'd be damned if Bex was intimidated for even a single second on a campus that we ruled over. That was completely unacceptable.

Cheers sounded around me, and students called out my name, trying to congratulate me, but I was up the stairs and to our private box within seconds. Breaker swung open the door, looking unsurprised at my arrival.

"Oh! Gage!" Bexley snapped around, plastering a smile on her face and looking thrilled to see me. "I didn't see you on the field; I was so confused. Congratulations on winning! I don't understand rugby super well, but you did amazing—" She stopped mid-sentence, her smile dropping. "Wait, what's wrong?"

Her brow dipped as I approached her as slowly as I could, not wanting to throw her off by the intensity coming off me at the idea of my mate being threatened. When I reached her, I cupped her jaw, examining her darkened gold eyes, a rumble breaking from my throat in frustration at her small attempt to shield her emotions from me.

"What happened? Why was security up here?"

"Oh." She drew her bottom lip in. "That was nothing, they just said—"

"Professor Clanguard wants to talk to the four of us," Jagger said, the indifferent look on his face not matching the power that his dragon was forcing through the room in a turbulent storm. Normally my dragon would be defensive about the idea of another dragon trying to assert dominance, but for once he was silent, aware we were all united under the need to figure out what had upset Bexley and how we could make her happy once more.

"What the hell does he want?" I bit out, glaring at the field. If he'd wanted to have a meeting then he could have discussed it with me instead of sending security to bother my mate. I didn't care if he was a powerful alpha—or would-have-been alpha—or the sector leader. I didn't give a shit.

Until recently, I had been the one to upset Bexley and now that we had some semblance of peace and security, the truth of our connection wrapping around us, I would do anything to maintain that. To keep her happy.

"No idea. Probably has to do with Ioan, if I had

to guess. Some of the other students confronted her about what happened," Breaker growled.

"I let them," Bexley added softly, her hand rubbing against my chest. It didn't bother me that Bexley wanted to answer their questions—although she didn't need to—but she was a fairly transparent and forward person, so it didn't surprise me, and it was her truth to share if she wanted.

What bothered me was that anyone thought it was okay to approach her in the first place.

I had never considered what it would be like to be a female dragon at this school—well, until the reality of others knowing Bexley's identity hit me in the face. As a male dragon, specifically a storm dragon, there was an innate sense of power, especially in a closed shifter society like our sector. But I had a feeling that being a female dragon would bring an entirely new set of struggles that I hadn't even begun to imagine.

Like people thinking they had a right to question her.

"Where do we need to meet him?" I tried to keep calm despite everything telling me to bash the bastard's face in. He was only leaving the field now, after having continued to stare at me for a long moment, wanting me to go back down there. As team captain of the victors, I knew he would want me to give some statement to the sector, but that wasn't going to happen. If they wanted someone to give a statement to report back to the rest of Trabea, then he could be the one to do so.

"His on-campus house," Jagger answered.

I paused. *That was unusual.* In fact, with the exception of his brother, I had never heard of anyone going anywhere near to the place. He clearly wanted to talk about something serious.

"Fine," I muttered and looked down at Bexley. "You look absolutely beautiful, cupcake. Thank you for coming to cheer me on." I knew that it couldn't have been easy. Even now, as students left the stadium, I was on high alert, feeling gazes move our way. I was thankful that it was so damn loud because with shifter hearing, I'm sure there were still some who could hear the details of our conversation—although hopefully not most.

"I just wish you were more excited for the win," she said. "I feel like I'm ruining it with all this serious nonsense. I'm really not even upset, just surprised and a bit confused." She paused and exhaled, her brow furrowing and betraying her concern. "What do you think he wants to talk about?"

"Probably the fact that you shifted," I said. And all the implications that came with not only with her being a female dragon, but mated to three storm dragons. It was damn near unheard of. Before all of the suspicion and mistrust, I think our families had an idea that it was a possibility when we were older, especially with how close all of us were, but I had never fully asked.

"Alright." She exhaled nervously. "Let's get it over with."

Unfortunately, I didn't think it would go nearly as fast as we all hoped for.

After waiting a few minutes for the crowd to clear, we made our way back to the dorm. Once there, Jagger and Breaker stayed downstairs with Bexley as she explored the perimeter of the forest around us, familiarizing herself with the sector and leaving her own scent on it as she trailed her fingers over each leaf and branch, although I didn't think she realized that was what she was doing.

I knew that despite being blocked from her shifted side, she'd still retained many natural shifter abilities like enhanced sight and hearing, but I had a feeling stronger ones would be returning to her now. More animalistic and confusing ones, like the need to scent her new home and even her mates. I wanted nothing more than to have my scent all over Bex, and I very much wanted her to feel similar, even if it wasn't the most logical thought.

After showering and changing quickly, I came

downstairs to find Bexley pointing to an area of damp earth in between Breaker's dorm and her own. "I'm telling you, *this* is the perfect place for it."

"For what?" I asked curiously.

"A garden," she hummed happily. "Of course I know nothing about gardening, but I miss the flowers every day. Maybe we could have some here."

Jagger, the proud bastard, was instantly smiling despite not taking credit for the flowers she received daily. I wanted to say something, but it was his moment to have whenever he decided to tell her, so instead I suggested, "Why don't we have them add some garden beds? It's a bit too late in the year to do it now, but maybe for the spring?"

"We could have someone from the witch sector put a protective spell on them to last through the cold months," Breaker suggested.

"Can they really do that?" Her eyes went wide.

"Magic can be handy." I mused, already imagining a greenhouse we could construct for her. "Although our magic isn't nearly as cool as theirs."

"I mean, you can fly, Gage. That's pretty cool."

"*We* can fly," Jagger corrected.

"Right—*we*." Bexley grinned but quickly deflated. "Crap. I was going to suggest we do that now, but we really need to go to this meeting, don't we?"

"Yeah," I grunted in frustration. "Clanguard probably has a good reason in his mind, so we might as well. Plus there isn't much to do on campus on a Saturday now that the game is over, so we'll have plenty of time to see about the garden after."

"Unless we wanted to go to a party," Bexley said, her gaze moving back towards the ground as if examining it further. The way she suggested it was light and indifferent enough, but I didn't buy it.

My brows went up. "What?"

"Figured there may be parties going on." She offered me an innocent smile before tilting her head in confusion. "Isn't that what students do on the weekend—party?"

"Or knit and watch movies with their three dragon mates," I suggested hopefully. I could already see the sparkling excitement in her eyes, though. I had a feeling Bexley was bringing this party up as more than just a casual suggestion.

I couldn't blame her completely—outside of events at the Bronzeheart estate, Bexley hadn't attended many social events, so if she wanted to go, we would have to make that happen without losing it...

Or maybe convince her that knitting was a better option. Fuck. I was going to try to keep my shit together, especially now that she knew the truth, but

I wasn't positive just how much my dragon could deal with. The idea of other male shifters looking at her made me see red.

"There are parties," Jagger admitted. "Just not positive they're the parties you should be at. They'll be filled with a lot of people that would probably cause their fair share of problems."

"I still wouldn't mind seeing them," Bexley hedged. *Yeah, my cupcake really wanted to go.*

"Then we will," Breaker said easily before transitioning our conversation, ignoring the glare that Jagger shot his way. "Come on, let's see what Clanguard wants."

The walk to the faculty on-campus housing wasn't far, the reasonably sized matching houses forming a semi-circle around a lake. It was quiet and peaceful, most faculty out enjoying their day off. As we made our way towards the house on the far left, following Clanguard's familiar scent, I noticed it unsurprisingly featured the most land.

The wolf shifter was a territorial bastard —shocking.

Before we could even reach the door, Clanguard opened it and I saw relief fill his gaze, making me wonder if he'd thought we wouldn't show up.

"I tried to call you over to explain," Clanguard said, clearly frustrated at having to explain himself.

"Security wasn't supposed to say anything until I'd already talked to you."

"Well, they clearly didn't listen," Jagger bit out.

"And I apologize for that," Clanguard said, stepping back and motioning for us to enter. "Bexley, I'm sorry if the incident caused you undo concern. That wasn't my intention."

I was glad he had the sense to apologize to her.

As we walked through the door into the house, my mate offered him a small smile. "It's no problem, seriously."

Upon entering, I immediately took stock of the space, listening for anyone else and scenting only two people other than Clanguard, one being Fletcher and the other unknown. They weren't here right now, but they had been recently.

"Oh, Rachel has been here!" Bexley perked up, and I watched as Clanguard's ears turned deep red. He let out a grunt but didn't respond, continuing to lead us forward to what I had to assume was his home office.

"Did I say something wrong?" Bexley asked me softly when he didn't respond, telling Breaker something about an upper level class instead.

"Never," I murmured, wondering if I should call him on his shit for worrying Bex. "He's just not supposed to be with a student."

My cupcake's eyes went wide, nodding in understanding as we entered his office. He rounded the desk, and the three of us spread out through the room. Jagger stood by the window, Breaker paced along the back, and I sat on an armchair with Bexley on my lap. As a group we took up as much space as possible, not fully on purpose, but our dragons instinctively didn't like being in wolf territory. Even if it was just Clanguard's house, it put me on edge.

I trusted him, but the pack he would have been alpha of had a history of human rights abuses and other horrible stuff. Their current alpha, his and his brother's father, was a piece of shit.

"What did you call us here for?" I asked as my cupcake leaned back into me. I liked having her here, right within grasp, safe and sound.

"Ioan. This is partly about what happened with him," Professor Clanguard explained, seemingly distracted. "I understand he attacked you, Bexley, and that's what caused your shift?"

I would've asked how he knew Ioan had attacked her, but he was a professor, and I knew surveillance was big in the sector.

"Yes." Bexley wrung her hands together nervously. "I didn't mean to shift, but he was choking me—" Panic caught her voice, and my chest squeezed uncomfortably. Clanguard nodded in

M. Sinclair

understanding, looking upset, and I found myself respecting him more for not even questioning her story or pushing it when she didn't continue.

"I'm sure you won't be surprised to find that this isn't the first time that rumors of Ioan's actions have reached me. But this time, since it comes with multiple witnesses, I've had him removed from school. He's not expelled yet—it's not my decision—but I wanted to assure you that he is off campus and far away from you. I hope that gives you a bit of peace."

"It does," Bexley breathed out.

"How does the Arnoult family feel about that?" Jagger asked with disdain. "I can't imagine they're happy about how this is playing out." I didn't recognize Ioan's family name, but if I had to guess from Jagger's tone, it seemed they were as bad as their offspring.

"Unhappy, of course." Clanguard sighed before looking at me. "They won't push, though, because she's listed as Bexley Bronzeheart."

I fucking loved that way too much. I could practically sense the frustration from Jagger and Breaker at my last name next to hers, but I only felt slightly bad for that.

"They don't know much about her," Clanguard continued, "but now that they're aware she's a dragon and under your clan's protection, they will view her as untouchable."

"Good," Breaker rumbled.

"I had to contact the Bronzehearts because they're your guardians," Clanguard explained to Bexley. "School policy. So they're aware you've shifted."

"Oh wow." Bexley's gaze shifted down. "I imagined telling them myself, but okay."

"They know," I murmured into her hair, reminding her that my parents had been aware of her being a dragon this entire time. Bexley relaxed.

"And they're planning to come tomorrow," Clanguard concluded.

I offered an arched brow. It didn't surprise me that my parents were coming, but I was confused why they hadn't called us home instead.

"They were the only two families informed, correct? The Bronzehearts and Arnoults?" Jagger asked.

"Yes. Neither of your families were contacted, although my understanding is that Bexley is your...mate?"

"It's not your business, but yes," I growled, unable to help myself. I hated the idea of anyone thinking about Bexley mating. I knew I was being ridiculous, which was evidenced by Clanguard's annoyed expression, but instead of fighting me on it, he just looked down at his desk in thought.

I had to admit, I was impressed he had such control over his animal. If another alpha snapped at me the way I was at him, I probably wouldn't take it nearly as lightly.

"You're right, it's not." He exhaled. "Thankfully that was the worst of the news. The next part is a bit easier."

Bexley tilted her head curiously. "What's the next part?"

"Your schedule." He offered her a folder, and my smile grew. This was an aspect I hadn't considered, all the changes that her shift would result in academically.

"My schedule? I have a schedule already."

"You shifted into a dragon, cupcake. You have a new schedule and new classes."

"Oh," she whispered and stood, taking the folder from him.

"*This* is different," Bexley said as she opened it, examining the paper with slight nervousness in her voice. I had a feeling that Clanguard had put her in classes that coincided with ours as much as possible. He may have been a professor, but as a shifter, he'd understand exactly the type of situation we were in and the instinctual urge to be around your mate as much as possible.

I squeezed her waist as I stood. "You've got this, cupcake."

Especially with us by her side.

Chapter Six

Bexley

"Well that wasn't nearly as bad as I assumed," I murmured to myself while unzipping my boots and putting them away in my closet. Deciding to get changed into something comfortable, I pulled on a pair of gold velvet pants and a matching zip jacket. It was one of my favorites, and while these tracksuits weren't particularly popular anymore, especially in the human realm, I still loved them and had practically hoarded them.

Especially the ones with bedazzled words on the butt. There was just something so fun and glittery about them. Plus, every time I wore them Gage had some sort of comment on them, which of course had fed my fantasy that he was looking at my butt.

Although that wasn't a fantasy anymore, was it?

Walking into the living room to take a closer look at my new schedule, a groan broke from Breaker's throat where he was making a snack. "*Mo chuisle,* do those pants say—"

"Juicy? On her ass? Yeah, they do," Gage grumbled, making me smile. He had always disliked these pants. Well, I'd *thought* he disliked them... Now I realized he probably didn't like me wearing them out because he was possessive. But still, when I mentioned getting rid of them, joking more than anything, he bought me ten more sets.

So yeah, he didn't dislike them at all. Lesson learned.

"They're so comfy!" I exclaimed as I picked up the folder and sat next to Jagger. His lips pressed up in amusement, but his eyes were dark with heat as his large hand wrapped around my shoulder, pulling me into his side.

I could hear Breaker and Gage lamenting over how I shouldn't be able to wear the pants I had on, but I mostly tuned it out because all my attention was on the new classes I would be taking, something that both intrigued me and made me nervous. I had just been getting used to my current ones!

"I like them on you." Jagger nipped my ear, pulling me out of my anxious musings.

Tilting my head slightly, I looked up at him and

let out a soft surprised moan as he pressed his lips to mine without any hesitation. Despite being slightly quieter and more reserved than the others, Jagger never hesitated to touch me when we were together, and I absolutely loved it. It helped remove any possible insecurities when it came to our relationship.

"Alright," Gage rumbled, sitting down. "Let's look at this schedule."

Jagger broke away and shot him a frustrated look, causing me to giggle as I leaned further into him. Despite their occasional frustrations with each other, I could tell the three of them were best friends. And now that I knew the truth, it felt like the tension had been reduced greatly, allowing me to see how easily I could get used to this. Get used to this level of peace and comfort from being surrounded by them.

A moment later Breaker joined us, setting down a plate of small sandwiches. I grabbed one and took a bite, his eyes filling with satisfaction. I wasn't sure if Breaker normally cooked often—the others didn't seem to find it odd—but I could tell that it made him happy when I ate his food, and it was always delicious, so I had absolutely no complaints.

"Alright," I said, holding out the paper. "So on Monday I still have *Dark Imaginarium Academy History & Basics* with Clanguard. Which is good since Rachel is in that one, and I wouldn't want to lose that class with her, especially since we're already paired up for class projects. But then later that day—"

"*Developing Bonds with your Animal Counter-part*," Jagger said, looking over my shoulder. "It's a more advanced version of *Understanding & Communicating*. Makes sense since you are a predatory shifter—they tend to go a different route with that. It's also nice because we help with that class."

"You do?" I asked eagerly, relief filling my chest. New classes with upperclassmen sounded intimidating, but if my mates were there? Not nearly as bad.

"Yeah, it should be mostly sophomores," Gage said, "but the teacher, Professor Tag, has been working with us privately for some classes since we got here. So we come in to help when we can."

"So I get to see you in my class," I concluded happily. "I love that."

"What's Tuesday?" Breaker asked curiously.

"*Hierarchy in Shifter Dominance* still, but later that afternoon it looks like there is a 'free gym' type thing? I'm scheduled for that on Thursday, too."

"Once you're a junior or a high-level shifter," Gage said, "you're given time in the sector to shift and run or fly as you please. Tuesdays and Thursdays are our times to shift if we want to. It ensures less run-ins, especially when less dominant shifters take flight." *That actually made a lot of sense.* "We don't always use that time, but it's nice to have it."

I liked the idea of shifting with them more than once a week, so maybe they would want to start using the time more if it was with me. I didn't understand the dynamic yet of how often they shifted or how it affected the other students, but I knew it wasn't done lightly.

Focusing back on the schedule, I drew my finger to Wednesday. "So the next day it says I now have *Shifting Under Attack* instead of *Shifting with Ease*."

"We're in that class as well. He didn't have to put you in that, but I'm glad he did," Breaker said, placing another sandwich in my free hand. I didn't think he purposefully did it, either. It seemed like a subconscious action.

"Do they expect us to be under attack often?" I murmured to myself while taking a bite, but Jagger chuckled softly. It wasn't a completely carefree laugh, though; there was tension in his frame. Probably because we had just been talking yesterday about how my family had been attacked.

It was odd knowing that there had possibly been a target on my back this entire time without me realizing it. I was really hoping it wasn't one of the other clans, not because I was worried about my own safety, but because I didn't want one of my mates to go through the pain I knew that would cause if that were the case.

"Thursday is still *Handling Animalistic Urges* and that free flight time," I said, trying to move on mentally, "and Friday is *History of Trabea*."

"So overall not that much different than it was before," Gage observed, causing me to relax a bit. He was right. There may have been a few changes, but they were changes I could deal with.

"Enough of a change that we get to see one another in some of my new classes," I hummed happily. "Plus Rachel will still be in a good amount of my classes."

"I have a feeling her schedule may change soon as well," Gage mused.

"Why?" I asked, closing my folder and finishing my second mini-sandwich.

"She's his mate. He's probably going to want to put her in classes he teaches, even if he shouldn't, and I have to assume she's Fletcher's mate as well," Jagger said, making me pause. I wasn't completely surprised by that revelation, but I hadn't put that together fully until now.

"Fletcher mentioned how it would be hard to share a mate with his brother since he teaches here..." I drew out.

Gage rumbled, drawing my attention. I swear the man was nearly pouting at Fletcher's name.

I offered him an understanding smile. "Hey, seriously, Fletcher is a friend, and if he's Rachel's mate, then he is really a friend."

"I'm sure he's okay," Gage muttered, "although I haven't interacted with him a lot. My main issue besides him staying away from our mate—"

Jagger made a sound of agreement, and I had a feeling that it was because Gage used 'our' instead of 'mine.' It was a subtle shift I loved.

"—is that he's from the Clanguard pack. They're ruthless assholes."

"Well, they both seem okay," I said, and then I sat up straighter in excitement. "Wait! Could we do a double—well, it would be more than double, I guess—date thing? That sounds super fun to me. Or would that not work since he's a teacher?"

"I'm sure we can figure it out," Breaker said, and Jagger kissed the side of my head, both of them chuckling. I was completely serious though. I wanted to celebrate Rachel and me finding our mates. Although I guess 're-finding' mine would be more accurate.

"Actually, I would love to see Rachel tonight." I grabbed a third sandwich. "Any idea if she would go to one of the parties tonight? Could we ask? I don't have her number, so how do I reach her?"

"I could get in touch with Fletcher," Gage said. "All the alphas on campus have phones from back home."

"Although we rarely use them," Jagger murmured. "As for parties...that sounds like there would be a lot of males there."

"But also a lot of fun if we go together." I grinned at him. "Come on, doesn't an entire group of people celebrating together sound fun? We even had a game today! I'm sure they're celebrating that."

"A group of people does not sound appealing to me," Jagger grumbled. "But if you want to go..."

"Then we can make it happen," Breaker agreed. "I feel better knowing that Ioan is off campus. I'm surprised his family isn't throwing more of a fit, especially since they're fairly well connected."

Breaker's words immediately jogged an important memory.

"I forgot to tell you!" I hopped up and turned to face them, all of them staring at me in concern. "When Ioan was...hurting me, he mentioned that he knew I'd been found in an alleyway. Said a bunch of mean stuff about it, but my bigger concern is that I have no idea how he found that out. I mean, unless

I'm crazy, I'm almost positive your parents have kept that quiet, Gage."

Gage's gaze grew more bronze than green, darkening on the edges. "Yeah, there should be no way he knew that. Besides my parents and these two, no one else knows the exact details of that night."

"Not to mention that it fucking concerns me that he was looking into her," Breaker rumbled, his expression turning dark.

"Shit," Jagger cursed, running a hand through his hair. "We need to get a hold on what his friends know, especially because they were the bastards who got in our way when we tried to follow you, little treasure."

"Wait, what? They did?" My brows went up in surprise.

"We need to be on high alert. This has the potential to be a huge problem," Gage said before looking at me. "I don't want anyone looking into your past until we know who targeted your family."

Before knowing the truth, I would've thought that he didn't want anyone knowing the Bronzehearts had taken in someone of such meager beginnings, but any of those insecurities had been diminished in the light of what had been revealed. More so, it was an irrational thought because the Bronzehearts were such good people that I had absolutely no doubt they would have taken any child under their wing if they found them in an alleyway, heir or not.

"Okay." I agreed, wanting to ensure we handled this the right way.

"As for his friends," Jagger bit out, "when we went to follow you, not wanting you to get too far, his friends stepped in front of us and tried to cause a problem. We tried to resolve it peacefully—" Which was sweet because I was almost positive they were only doing that for me. "— but the minute you screamed, it was over."

I remembered screaming. I remembered the pain at my first shift in so long, the only one I could remember.

I squeezed his hand, and his arm tightened around me. "Thank you for trying to handle it peacefully." Turning my attention to the others, I added, "Maybe...maybe we should look into his friends. I don't want anyone at risk because of my past."

"So damn sweet," Breaker murmured, making my cheeks heat.

"It may take a bit of convincing to get them to tell us," Jagger said softly.

"Convincing?" I arched my brow.

"Violence. It may take violence," Breaker admitted.

Oh.

"Which is why the two of us are going to go to a party," Gage grunted, standing and nodding towards Jagger and Breaker. "They'll handle it. You are going to relax and have some fun."

"And you'll relax with me?" I asked hopefully. I wanted all three of them to be able to come with me, but it was clear they had a plan in mind.

"As much as I can." He flashed a knowing smile.

"Next time I'm going with her," Jagger rumbled.

"Bexley." Breaker came up and cupped my cheek. "I promise we will try to handle it as nonviolently as possible, but we need to know if they're a threat."

"I understand," I said, standing and kissing him briefly. I turned towards my room. "I'm going to get ready! Don't you two leave yet, I want to say goodbye!"

And give each of them a kiss.

"Oh, I plan on waiting—I need to know what these other males are going to be seeing you wearing," Jagger rumbled.

Breaker chuckled. "I love everything she wears."

"Yeah, I love her outfits too much—that's the problem," Gage pointed out.

Well...if they loved them that much, I would keep wearing them.

Chapter Seven

Bexley

"It's beautiful out," I said to Gage as we stepped outside, leaving the dorm behind us. Most of the morning had been rather chilly, but the evening air had settled into a far more comfortable temperature, making my boots, skirt, and sweater combination the perfect choice. Even if my three mates had grumbled about it a little bit.

Apparently, despite being completely covered up, it was a sexy outfit. I mean, I wouldn't complain if they thought so. Then again, I was starting to think they found everything I wore attractive. It was extremely flattering.

"It is. Can you smell the storm coming?" Gage asked, gently running a hand over my back. His scent was all around me, but so were Jagger's and Breaker's, though theirs were more of a faint trace. I had a feeling, especially with the way they'd kissed me before we left, that it had been more than a bit purposeful.

Closing my eyes momentarily, trying to search past their familiar scents, I inhaled as Gage led me down an unfamiliar path that went towards the west side of campus. I paused my even pace as I caught the slight scent of ozone, snapping my eyes open and giving Gage a quick nod. Satisfaction filled his face.

As intimidating as the concept of being a storm dragon was, I loved everything it meant that Gage and I could share in now. Everything that I would have in common with my mates.

"I can't wait to go flying in a storm together, cupcake," he rumbled, urging me forward. "You're going to love it."

"I would love any chance to fly with you," I admitted. "I'm bummed that I can't remember this last time, especially since the three of you were in the air with me." It was something I wanted a repeat of as soon as possible.

"We have a lot of time coming up, I promise." Gage squeezed my hand and pulled me to a stop as we heard voices up ahead. I went up on my toes, seeing a slight glow from the trees and hearing the low murmur of voices and music, broken only by laughter or someone shouting. Excitement rolled through me as I looked back at Gage, who was staring ahead as if there was a potential threat.

"What?" I asked softly, suddenly considering the concept, especially with what happened with Ioan.

"Just trying to get a sense of who's there, but it seems to mostly be upperclassmen," he said. "Possibly some aquatic shifters."

"How can you tell that?" I asked in surprise.

Instead of answering, he looked down at me, concern shading his gaze. "You're sure you want to go?"

"Hmmm," I teased, bringing my finger to my chin in thought. "I mean, unless you would rather go back to the dorm and knit..."

"I would absolutely rather do that."

"Nope!" I sang in amusement and turned out of his grip, walking backwards on the path and trying to hide my growing smile at his obvious grumpiness. I did notice there was a distinctly dark way he watched me, almost predatory in nature, and I absolutely loved it.

"Bexley, come back here," Gage rumbled.

"Can't do that. Don't trust that you won't drag me back like some freakin' cave dragon." I flashed him a smile and turned to speed-walk down the path, groaning playfully as he suddenly appeared behind me. One large hand splayed over my stomach and the other knotted my hair around his fist as he tilted my head back, heat and amusement warring in his gaze.

"Cave dragon—that's a new one," he rumbled and leaned down, nipping my lip.

"I thought it was funny," I murmured, sighing happily.

"It is funny—funny enough that you should tell me more about it...back in the dorms."

"Gage." I pulled back from his lips, and he muttered a curse but kissed me lightly before releasing me.

"I know. We're going, just need to keep my shit together," he rumbled.

"That'll be easy," I insisted, grabbing his hand as we made our way towards the party.

***

I was wrong. It was *not* easy.

Mostly because his dragon was worked up by the fact that I was more than slightly miffed. In fact, I was starting to understand why my mates didn't have many friends, and it wasn't because they were inherently unfriendly. No, it was because other shifters were objectively terrified of offending them, or in this case, their mate. Me.

I hadn't noticed it at first, and when we got to the party, I had been so caught off guard by the sight of so many students gathered and relaxing together—a much more casual vibe than the other party I'd gone to—that I hadn't realized when the tone of the party significantly changed because of Gage's presence.

Students were literally moving away from us, and it wasn't long before we were cozying up, leaning against a tree on the outside of the gathering, no one taking the risk of approaching us.

"Sort of isolating, the fear element," I murmured, my brow dipping.

Gage let out a long exhale. "I don't mind it all that much, but it is frustrating. You either have fear or the other option—some bastard trying to challenge you."

I took a sip of my wine Gage had gotten me from the nearby bar. "If someone ever challenged me... Actually, I don't think I would realize they were challenging me."

My body shook as Gage barked out a laugh, kissing my shoulder. Unfortunately, before he could say anything, a figure walked around from the left and approached us, their deep voice filling the space. "Well, then you would not only lose, but most likely die."

I froze, surprised by his cold, unflinching analysis

as Gage let out a deep, dangerous sound from the back of his throat. The student didn't seem bothered by it, though, and when he stepped into the light from the bonfire nearby, my brows rose in surprise. I wasn't sure what I'd expected from the smooth voice, but it wasn't him.

He was large, surprisingly so with how quiet he moved, but he was also extremely stocky, like four times my width. He had bulky muscles that were mostly covered in dark clothes, but from what I could see of him, namely his face, he was covered in thin battle scars. The most unique feature about him, though? His eyes were completely black. There were no whites to them, and it left me with an eerie feeling as he stared at me.

"Talk about my mate dying again and I'll break every bone in your body."

I stilled as my gaze snapped up to Gage, who was staring at the man with pure malice and disdain. I had no idea who this guy was, but I had a feeling Gage really didn't like him, and not just because he'd talked about me dying.

"I meant no harm; it's just the truth, especially if she was challenged," he offered, bringing my attention back. "Which she will be."

"Why?" I frowned in confusion.

"Erty, I highly suggest you don't start anything

you can't finish," Gage warned. *Erty*. Was that his name?

Erty grimaced, putting his hands out in an innocent gesture. "Just trying to give you a heads-up. There are a lot of dominant female shifters that don't like their position being challenged by a female dragon. She needs to watch her back."

"Wait, really?" I asked softly.

Gage shook his head in frustration. "Bexley will not be fighting. That's final." He said it with such finality, but despite his confidence, I could see a nervous edge to his posture. Gage was never nervous.

"A challenge is a challenge," Erty expressed. "I know a few people from my own group who plan on it. I'm not the judge to say if it's right or wrong, just figured I would give another alpha some forewarning."

Then he was gone.

"Fucking shark shifters," Gage grunted before sweeping me off my feet and walking away from the party. I knew others were looking at us and probably had heard the convo, but I was far more caught up on not only his reaction but the all-important...shark shifter element? Holy crap. That was a thing?

That was a dumb question. Of course I knew there were aquatic shifters, I just had never imagined them. In fact, we'd never really focused on other types of shifters besides the most common ones, like wolves, bears, deer... And now I had to wonder why. From only the few interactions we'd had, I was getting the distinct impression there were issues between the aquatic shifters and the dragon clans.

"What's wrong? I mean, what he said isn't that surprising," I pointed out.

Now that we were far enough away from the party that it was a dim light in the distance, Gage pressed me up against a tree and buried his nose against my neck, holding me hostage. I could tell he was trying to calm himself down before answering, so instead of pushing it, I ran my hands through his hair in what I hoped was a comforting movement.

"It's the challenge aspect."

"What about it? If they challenge me, I'll just say no," I offered, trying to keep it lighthearted. Gage shook his head and pulled back, letting me slide down his body as his hand came up to cup my jaw.

"That's the issue—if someone issues a formal challenge for dominance, you can't say no. If you do, they still have a right to attack you. It's either that or you have to submit to them."

"What the heck? Why in the fates would I do either of those things? Why does it matter? It's not like I'm going to go around asking them to do anything, why would there need to be a challenge to begin with?"

"I know it doesn't make sense, but Erty's right. Other female shifters, specifically those who consider themselves alphas, will want to challenge you."

I stared up at him, realizing that he was authentically concerned about what would happen. I drew in my lip. "And you're worried I'd get hurt if I fought them?"

Gage snorted. "No." A part of me, most likely my dragon, relaxed, not liking the idea of him seeing us as weak. "The opposite, Bexley. You may not be violent, but if you're threatened, your dragon will act accordingly, and I know you don't want to hurt anyone."

My smile grew, unable to help myself because despite the circumstances, what he was saying was actually really sweet.

"Well," I drew out, reaching up to run my hand over his chest. "I'll just explain that, then. I'll say I don't want to hurt them and suggest we leave it alone. I'm sure they'll listen."

Gage's gaze flashed with amusement as his scowl deepened, like he was trying to not find my words funny. I was serious though! I felt like I could appeal to most students' rationales here. I mean, who really wanted to fight if they didn't have to?

"If that works..." Gage groaned and chuckled. "You know what, cupcake, I wouldn't be surprised. You have a way with everyone that I will never understand."

"Yeah? I feel like I'm not the best at being social."

"People love you," Gage countered. "Look at how Erty came over to 'look out for you,' which makes no sense since half of his scars come from challenges he's issued himself. And then with Diane approaching you... It's very interesting."

"It's because they can tell I'm friendly," I said, flashing a big winning smile that had him chuckling. I saw the darkness fade from his gaze and immediately felt better. I didn't want him to worry about challenges or anything like that. We would figure it out, and I had to believe people were a bit more rational than he was assuming.

I mean, seriously. Who would want to fight a freakin' dragon!

"And beautiful and brilliant," Gage said, stepping into my space and brushing his lips against mine. Gage and I had always been touchy, but it was like a floodgate had been opened, and I was loving the unrestrained affection he was giving me.

His touch was soft and cautious though, like he

didn't want to kiss me too much, and when I tried to deepen it, he groaned and pulled away.

"Not here," he said, his gaze darting towards the party.

"They are so far away, and I guarantee no one is paying attention to us kissing," I teased as he ran a thumb over my lip.

"I don't want anyone hearing those sweet noises you make, cupcake."

My cheeks flushed bright red as I slipped around him and huffed. "Fine, fine! I get it." I looked back at him, flashing a smile as I walked in the opposite direction of the party. "You *clearly* don't want to kiss me—

"Gage!"

The minute the words were out of my mouth, Gage was on me, wrapping an arm around my waist and pulling my back flush with his chest, pinning me between his body and another large tree. He let out an actual growl, the sound vibrating through me as my toes curled in response, my breath catching.

"Bexley, if you walk away from me one more time—"

Something seemed to be roaming under his skin, almost a primal magic that rolled over me and had my blood pumping loudly in my ears. "What will you do?" I dropped my head back, my words meant to sound challenging but instead coming off breathy.

Instead of answering me, he brought his other hand up and wrapped it around my throat, dropping his lips to mine as I let out a soft, pleasure-filled moan. How had I gone so long without kissing him? I didn't understand how I'd survived without it.

"Mark you," he finally answered in a low rumble. "Mark you so that no matter where you go, cupcake, people will know who you belong to. So that no matter how far you run, you will always remember whose bite mark is on your neck."

I inhaled sharply, realizing he was talking about an official mating mark. "Gage—"

Letting out a pained sound, he tugged on my bottom lip. "But I can't do that without being inside of you. I don't have that type of control."

"I don't like control," I whispered, unable to stop myself. His gaze snapped to mine and flashed pure bronze.

"Bexley," he warned. I let out a small whimper and pressed my butt back against him, feeling his hard length. His hand that had been around my waist slid down and back up, pushing up my skirt as his fingers gripped my thigh, their rough texture causing my center to grow far more wet.

Only my three mates had the power to turn me

on like this. I felt like a different woman in their arms, and my body recognized it, my skin flushing in response to the simple yet intensely possessive touch.

"I'm serious, I want your mark," I admitted, my voice uneven. I didn't know fully what I was asking for—I didn't know a lot about dragon mating—but I knew I wanted him more than my next breath.

Gage pressed his lips hard to mine, his fingers digging into my thigh before he shook his head. "No —I won't take you out here, not like this. I want our first time to be special."

It would be special, though.

"And more importantly, far away from any of these bastards," he growled softly.

That was a fair point.

"But that doesn't mean I'll leave you frustrated." Gage pulled back slightly and brought his hand around my throat to smooth over my lips. I whimpered in surprise as the hand on my thigh continued to push up my skirt until his fingers were trailing over the apex of my thighs, my silk panties soaked through.

"Gage," I moaned as he slid his fingers underneath the material, gasping as his thick fingers slid along my slit and circled my clit. My thighs were shaking from the tension and frustration, but I didn't push for more, worried that if I did he would take the touch away.

"I can't even tell you all the times I thought about doing this, pushing up one of these damn skirts you wear and burying my face against this sweet pussy. Fuck, Bex."

Before I could ask him to do just that, I moaned as he slid a thick digit inside of me. My eyes fluttered shut, feeling damn near euphoric at the attention he was paying my body. My abdomen was tight, and I couldn't help but press further back, wanting his fingers as deep inside of me as possible.

"Or pumping my fingers in and out of you like this," Gage growled against my ear and began to do exactly that. My knees went weak, and my hands shot out to brace myself against the tree, but Gage had me locked against him. I wasn't going anywhere, and I loved it. I loved feeling trapped by him. I loved giving him every ounce of control.

"Better yet," he snarled, his lips moving down my neck, "imagining pounding in and out of you, filling you with every inch of my cock as I bury my teeth inside of your neck—"

"Gage!"

My orgasm came like a tidal wave, Gage's hand catching my cry of his name, but only barely. My center exploded in heat, and molten liquid moved through every inch of me, my heart beating a million miles an hour. My creature let out a satisfied purr as Gage groaned, his lips skimming against my neck and causing chills to roll over my skin.

"So damn responsive." He sounded pained as he pulled his fingers from me and knelt down behind me to adjust my skirt. I swayed slightly, over-whelmed, because for so damn long I had wanted his touch, and now that I had it...

"Fuck, you taste good," he rumbled after he'd licked my wet heat from his fingers, scooping me up in his arms. I tried to smile up at him, feeling dazed as my cheeks turned bright red in response to his action. I pressed my face against his neck, trying to hide my reaction. Though after what we had just done, it was ridiculous to feel shy right now..

"I'm ready to go home and knit now," I stated softly. "Unless you think we should go back to the party..."

He chuckled, tightening his hold on me. "You must be crazy if you think I'd let you go back to that party smelling like this. You are so sweet—you're fucking edible, Bexley."

Maybe it wouldn't take much convincing to get him to eat me up then.

Chapter Eight

Bexley

"I'll be ready in five minutes!" I promised, shouting out over the sound of my bathroom door slamming shut, the loud noise making me wince. Breaker's chuckle filled the other room, making me smile before I caught myself and scowled. He found it amusing that I was running around in a tiny panic.

I may or may not have forgotten that Gage's parents would be showing up here today, and Gage had woken me up only a few minutes ago saying that he was going to meet them at the entrance of the sector and bring them here.

I'd sat there, staring at him in surprise while trying to process his words, before I let out a panicked noise and ran to my closet to find something to wear. Of course I'd asked him why in the heck he hadn't woken me up earlier, frustrated at being so unprepared for such important guests, but then the man had said the sweetest thing that melted away any of that annoyance. He said he'd wanted me to get as much rest as possible.

Still, it left me with literally zero time to get ready!

I may have lived with the Bronzehearts most of my life, at least the years I could remember, and sure, they'd seen me in all different states, from half-asleep on Christmas morning to all dolled up for an event, but I wanted to appear at least somewhat put together since they were coming to visit me at the academy. I wanted them to see that I was managing being away from the estate just fine, even with all the big changes that'd been occurring.

Like shifting.

Gage had reminded me twice now that his parents had been well aware of my heritage—I mean, they'd been a fundamental part of my childhood, apparently—but it still felt like a big announcement, which left me feeling nervous.

That wasn't even including the fact that everyone seemed to be ignoring that we had to tell them we were mates. Unless, of course, they already knew that too...

I frowned, rubbing a hand over my face and

trying to push the negative thoughts from my head. I just didn't want to cause them any unnecessary problems. I mean, clearly I was causing a stir if they felt the need to come here, and I hated the idea of disrupting their life.

Washing my face quickly and then brushing my teeth, I pulled my hair back into a french twist before quickly changing into a light purple sweater dress, the soft material hugging my body comfortably. I'd gotten a night of deep sleep surrounded by two of my mates, but I was feeling a bit hazy after the past few days.

So much had happened, and I had a feeling that there was much more to come. I'd wished for clarity on my past for so long, but this was a bit more intense than I'd expected. Still, I was eager to see the Bronzehearts.

While I hadn't brought it up to my three mates, I was hoping Gage's parents would help fill in some of the blanks about my parents and my personal history. I wanted to know as much as possible, especially since there was the chance that Ioan, and even Ioan's friends, knew more about my past than they were letting on.

Then again, we didn't really know what they knew. When we'd gotten back to the dorm following the party, Breaker had been home, but Jagger hadn't.

Apparently he'd followed a different lead than Breaker, one that had kept him out a bit longer, much to my disappointment.

I'd been on edge, not wanting to fall asleep without Jagger being home, but Gage and Breaker had assured me that it would be fine. Luckily, only an hour later, after tossing and turning, Jagger strode in. I'd been pretty sleepy at that point, so I may have misremembered, but when he kissed me before saying he was going to change, I swore I caught the scent of blood.

But not his blood. I wasn't sure how I knew that, but I was positive it wasn't his.

I needed to ask him about that this morning, as well as the lead he followed, but I'd wait until *after* the Bronzehearts' visit for sure. My brain could only be tugged in so many different directions at once.

Once I was satisfied with my appearance, I pulled on a pale gold cardigan and walked out into the main room to find Jagger and Breaker talking by the kitchen, both of whom were dressed and had clearly been up for a few hours. But before I could say good morning, the sound of the elevator opening drew my attention and an excited smile broke onto my face.

Celine and Leopold Bronzeheart.

"Bex, honey!" In a second flat, Celine had me in

her arms, wrapped in an all-encompassing hug that had a small relieved sound breaking from my throat as I hugged her back.

A miniscule part of me that now knew I had another mom in my past, one who hadn't left me on the streets willingly but had instead tried to save me, wondered if I should feel guilty for viewing Celine as my mom. I'd always understood she wasn't truly my mom, biologically speaking, but that was who she'd been to me these past eight years. She'd been fundamental in forming the person I was today.

It was silly to feel any guilt, I knew that. I had no strong memories yet to even back up the other relationship, just a memory shrouded in mystery. And as I pulled back, examining her chocolate brown eyes brimming with maternal affection, it was clear that she viewed me as her daughter. She'd said it time and time again over the years, but now it was hitting home.

"I never should've let you leave home! That horrible boy attacked you in the first week! Bex, you must've been so scared." Tears leaked from her eyes as I nodded, unable to help the tears welling in my own. Of course I'd been scared, but up until now I'd been trying to be strong, to show my mates and even my fellow students that it wasn't something that could scare me off. It was ridiculous, but something about the fierceness mixed with the empathy in her expression made me so freakin' emotional.

She turned towards her husband, keeping me close. "I want him punished, Leo."

"I know," he said in understanding, "let's just take a moment to hear the full details—"

"No," Celine bit out, her voice laced with venom. "He attacked her, that's all I need to know. *He attacked our Bexley.* I will not see this unpunished."

Our Bexley. Considering how lost and confused I'd been feeling about my own past, her words filled me with a sense of security and relief. It wasn't that I thought the Bronzehearts would drop me now that I knew about my past, but it was still reassuring to hear that she viewed me as part of their family.

And right now, I would *not* want to be Ioan, who she viewed as a threat to her family. I'd always thought Leopold was the more intimidating member of Gage's family, but as I stared at Celine, I realized I may have been wrong. She may have been crying, but there was a strength and intensity radiating off of her, all on my behalf. It was beyond humbling.

"He's not on campus anymore, so I feel a lot better about that situation," I promised. Breaker made a low rumble in his throat, drawing my attention to his darkened expression on my tears. I hadn't realized it until this moment, but all three of my mates were staring at my tears in a bit of panic. I tried to blink them away, but I also didn't like the idea of hiding my emotions from them.

"We've been questioning his friends," Jagger explained. "Ioan mentioned something to her about knowing her past, at least the part about her being found in an alleyway, but so far we haven't been able to pin down if his friends know anything as well. They didn't seem to know anything extra about Bexley when I questioned them, though because of the specifics I couldn't ask directly."

Both Bronzehearts nodded in understanding. "Thank you for looking into that," Leopold said, exhaling and clapping his son's shoulder. "I'm glad the school called us. Ioan's family would've pursued this more directly if it wasn't for our name. They are always a fucking problem, and now we can handle it outside of the academy."

"And we will," Celine bit out. I tried to control my reaction, not because of the animosity in her voice, but because of Gage's father swearing. I didn't think I'd ever heard him do that before.

"I just don't want him back here." I pulled back slightly from her hold, squeezing her hand in reassurance. "I promise, I'm fine now. I don't want anyone else hurt. I just want him gone."

"He won't step foot back on this campus again, cupcake," Gage promised.

"Forever," Celine murmured, making my brows shoot up. She offered me a slightly embarrassed smile and wiped her eyes. "I'm sorry for the emotional outburst, but when I heard you were in trouble..."

"Thank you," I whispered. "Seriously, thank you. I was nervous about how you guys would react to all of this."

"Never be nervous. No matter what happened before you came to our estate, you will always have a place in our family," she vowed.

"She's right," Leopold added. "Always, Bex."

I nodded and let out a shaky breath.

As if realizing there were others in the room, Celine looked towards my mates, specifically Breaker and Jagger. "Boys! It's been so long—come give me hugs."

I watched with a goofy smile as she hugged both of them, their eyes wide in surprise. My gaze moved to Leopold, who was nearly smirking, his lips pressed up just enough that I knew he found the sight of his wife ordering hugs from them funny.

"I wish it hadn't been so long," Breaker admitted, looking at Leopold. "We've tried to keep things quiet from both of our families—we haven't mentioned that Bexley is alive."

"Although we have a suspicion that they know," Jagger hedged. "They've never talked about her in a grieving fashion—in fact, they haven't said anything at all. Which I would normally view as suspicious, but I don't get the feeling it's anything malicious."

Leopold nodded. "I would bet they know. Your parents aren't stupid."

"Which is why we have so much to talk about," Gage said motioning towards the living room, "and part of that is Bexley shifting—"

"Which is something to be celebrated." Leopold offered me a smile, holding my gaze with warmth. "Congratulations, Bexley. I'm sorry it was under those circumstances, but we've been trying for years to find a way to allow your magic to break out—"

"Careful!" Celine hissed.

"It's not painful anymore," I promised, realizing what the fear in her gaze was about. "We can talk about anything. My memories feel hazy, and not all of them have returned, but it's not painful. I can talk about being found that night in the alleyway, being a dragon, being mates with the three of them... None of it hurts to think about."

"Oh, thank the fates." Celine collapsed into a chair.

I had totally just slipped the mate thing in there,

and no one seemed to think it was odd, so I was going to assume they already knew?

Relief filled Leopold's gaze. "That's all we ever wanted. I'm sorry that we kept secrets from you—we never wanted to cause you pain, and seeing you so scared and in so much agony that night... Well, we did our best to avoid that at all costs."

"You're wonderful, both of you," I said seriously, feeling a surge of appreciation for how they'd handled the situation. If I had been found by anyone not as caring or careful, I imagine it could have been traumatic. The pain had been nothing to scoff at.

"What isn't wonderful..." Gage drew out, seemingly on edge with everything we needed to discuss, "is that everyone saw her shift. Everyone knows that she's a female dragon."

"But not what type," Jagger added.

"She needs to stay inside during storms," Leopold agreed. "At least until we move forward with our plan."

"Plan?" Breaker asked, his brow dipping. If they had a plan, it was making a bit more sense on why they had made a point of coming all the way here—besides checking on me.

"Which is truly why we're here," Leopold stated. "I wanted to talk about the prospect of the four of you coming to our estate this weekend so we can handle, in an official capacity, all of the news that is no doubt circulating through Trabea."

"We want to give the other clans the courtesy of officially knowing that you are alive and safe, Bex. We'll not only announce your identity, which will signify the return of the fourth ruling dragon clan, but also that the three of you share one mate."

They'd caught that then.

"Something I am so excited about!" Celine let out a happy hum. "Think about the wedding!"

"The...wedding," I whispered, less as a question and more a realization.

"Later." She winked.

"Are we sure this is a good idea?" Gage rumbled. "Announcing her so publicly?"

I didn't know what to make of their lack of a reaction to the wedding thing, all of them far more focused on the announcement portion. That was probably something we would need to talk about together, right?

"Yes. It will show unity and that even if the threat that hurt her family is still at large, she is under the protection of all three clans," Celine explained.

"As long as it wasn't one of our families," Jagger said easily, "something we've discussed extensively.

We presume that isn't the case since no one stepped forward to claim their land."

"Agreed." Leopold folded his arms. "The only potential problem with that is it'll make it clear what type of dragon she is."

"Everyone knows what type I was? Even when I was younger?" I asked curiously. I suppose that made sense—I'd always known Gage was a storm dragon.

"Oh, yes." Celine squeezed my hand. "There is so much I want to tell you, but because of the delicate nature of the topic and where we are, I want to wait until we're home to talk about your past. I have many memories to share with you as well as details on your clan and family. Is it okay if we wait?"

I nodded in excitement. I wanted to know everything there was to know, but I also understood that right now probably wasn't the best time to talk about it. I wanted to believe that this area was secure and that we would sense anyone close enough to listen, but better safe than sorry.

"That is going to put a massive target on her back," Breaker confessed, looking torn.

"She already has one," Leopold argued. "This way she'll have three clans behind her, as well as her own family name. Without that, she's a mystery. Enough of one to draw new attention, potentially including the people who targeted her family before. While they wouldn't definitively know the truth, it won't be hard for people to figure it out on their own. If we don't make the official announcement it will put her in more danger."

"I think I know what happened that night," I admitted out loud. "I don't know who, but I had a dream of when I was given my memory removal potion, and before that, the woman who did it—Rebecca—she said a name. I can't remember it, but I know I heard it in the dream, so eventually I will. She said I need to avoid that person at all costs."

The Bronzehearts exchanged a meaningful look before Leopold said, "Good, that's a place to start. If you and the boys are okay with it, we'd like to hold an official event as soon as possible. I would say this weekend, unless you'd like to come home sooner than that. We don't want accusations to start flying—the faster we handle this, the better. Luckily, Ioan's family is only well connected in the city, but I have no doubt news will reach the other two clans fairly quickly."

Both Jagger and Breaker nodded in agreement.

"I don't want to miss school," I admitted softly, conflicted on the idea of going back before the week-end. "But if you think it's necessary, we could try to leave after class tomorrow and come back by Tuesday? Would that work?"

"You may need to miss a day of class if we do it during the week," Celine said apologetically, "but let me make some calls and see what we can do. Gage, please keep in contact with us."

"You're leaving already?" I asked, feeling a surge of disappointment. I wanted them to stay.

"I know." Celine squeezed my hand. "But if we're going to have both clans come to our estate after so long, we need to make some calls. I promise we'll talk a lot more when you come home, we just needed to know you were okay and see it for ourselves. I also wanted to see your dorm, which I have to admit is far better than I expected."

"I think these three had something to do with that," Leopold mused.

All three of my mates were suspiciously quiet, making me tilt my head in thought as I looked around. It really was tailor-made for me.

After showing Celine around as the boys talked to Leopold, we took the elevator down with them and said goodbye. I felt emotional, wanting to follow them as they walked down the forest path, talking in relaxed and easy tones. I hadn't realized just how much I'd missed them until this moment.

"I promise we will see them soon," Gage said, running a hand over my waist. I sighed and nodded, but my attention was snagged suddenly by movement nearby.

When a small pink bunny hopped out from the bush, its fur the same shade as Rachel's hair, my eyebrows shot up. I moved forward and knelt down as it approached with a small note in its mouth.

"Rachel?" I asked softly. She dropped the note in my hand and ran, making my eyes widen. I could practically smell the fear coming off of her, making me wonder what had given her such a scare, and opened the note in hopes it would give me some clue.

Bex—

I tried to stop by for a visit, but there were so many dragons, my bunny forced me to shift because she was scared. I went back to my dorm and wrote this because I had a feeling it would happen if I tried to get close again.

I want you to know that I would love to still be partners. I know you have a lot going on, but if you want to work on our school project we can do it in the dining hall. I'll be there in about an hour!

Hope to see you soon.

—Rachel

. . .

"Yes! I'll be there!" I called out as I stood, hoping she was close enough to hear. Gage chuckled, and when I turned around, I found all three of them staring at me in confusion and a little amusement.

"Rachel brought me a note. She wants to work on our project, but her bunny forced her to shift because she was scared," I explained. "We're going to meet in the dining hall—you guys are welcome to come with us."

"Oh, we're coming with, little treasure," Jagger assured.

"Not leaving you alone," Breaker agreed as Gage kissed the top of my head.

Good. I always wanted my mates by my side.

Chapter Nine

Bexley

The walk to the dining hall was somewhat quiet, at least for me, as my thoughts went over everything the Bronzehearts had suggested.

Was I ready to be reintroduced to everyone? What backlash would they face for harboring me all these years? More so, what would Jagger and Breaker's parents think of me? What had they thought of me before? I wanted to ask my mates what their parents were like, but I was frustrated that I couldn't remember for myself.

"Alright, in you go, cupcake." Gage nodded towards the dining hall door.

I came to a stop, offering the three of them a confused look. "You aren't coming in with me?"

"Figured your friend would be a bit less nervous

without us right there. We're going to be right outside, and the doors are open so we can keep an eye on everything," Breaker said. I smiled softly at how thoughtful they were.

It was true that Rachel was nervous around them, and while I wanted to explain to her that there was no reason to be, that my mates were complete sweethearts, I was starting to understand that the fear was rooted deeply within the psyche of prey shifters, conforming to instinct rather than logic.

"This probably won't take long, but if you get tired of waiting out here, please join us," I said, already hating the idea of being away from them even if I knew I would have fun hanging out with Rachel.

"Of course." Jagger nodded, his gaze moving to the space between us as I took a step back. Offering a small, awkward wave that had all of them smiling, I turned towards the entrance of the dining hall, thankful it was mostly empty, making it easy to find my friend.

"Rachel!" I called as I made my way towards her, her blue eyes shooting to mine as she offered a small wave. I noticed that despite looking a bit timid and shy, she seemed excited to see me. Her pink hair was pulled into a messy, oversized bun, and she was wearing a large comfortable academy sweater.

I really freakin' needed to get something like that. Did they have a store for it? Or was it specially made? When I went home, I would ask Celine and try to get my hands on one. The woman had many talents, but procuring clothing seemed like a super-power the fates had blessed her with.

"I'm sorry about the weird bunny form of communication," Rachel huffed, tapping the seat next to her and pulling it out. "My bunny was terri-fied with all the dragons around—I'm not sure who was visiting, but six dragons was two too many."

"I completely understand." I didn't fully, but I was okay with whatever she was comfortable with. I didn't have a lot of experience with having girl-friends, but I didn't want her to be scared of my mates, or me, just because of the creatures we shifted into.

Sitting down, I put down my notebook and noticed that she had a ton of supplies on the table. I had to admit, I was impressed. Rachel struck me as someone who was always prepared...and then prepared some more.

"I'm just glad you still want to work together," I confessed. "I was nervous with having shifted and stuff that you wouldn't want to work with me anymore. People have been acting differently around me." I may have been blowing it out of proportion because I was hypersensitive to the negative attention, but even now I felt like people were staring at me, and not in a particularly nice way.

Her eyes went wide. "Of course I want to work with you, Bex. I was worried that you wouldn't want to work with me. But I know that's silly because you wanted to work with me before you even shifted."

"Because we're friends," I assured her. "Just because I'm a dragon and you're a bunny, it doesn't change anything.

"I love that." She nodded adamantly before her expression dipped into a frown. "I wish everyone thought like that."

"Oh!" I lowered my voice, her words triggering a thought. "So Professor Clanguard and Fletcher are your..."

"Yes," she squeaked out immediately, putting her hands on her cheeks as they flushed bright pink. "But don't tell anyone. I'm guessing your mates already know though."

I nodded and she huffed as if frustrated by people knowing, but not *actually* upset, if that made sense. "It's all so confusing, the entire situation. Fletcher says he wants to be with me but says that he doesn't want me around his family until he's in charge, which just feels like hiding me. I may be a bunny, a prey shifter for sure, but even to me it feels disrespectful. And then Thomas—sorry, Professor Clanguard—says we can't be together because of school, but with how he acts, you would never think that."

I took a minute to think over her words, loving that she was opening up and talking to me about everything. I hadn't expected it, and while I may not have had the best advice, it made me feel like our friendship was growing.

"How does he act?" I asked. I couldn't get a read on Professor Clanguard at all, truth be told. Sometimes he seemed extremely intimidating, and other times he seemed young, nearly our age.

"So freakin' possessive." Rachel shook her head and sighed. "Seriously, he makes me wear his academy sweaters around everywhere, and whenever I'm talking to a guy in a class he teaches—which isn't often, if at all—but when it does happen, he switches everyone's seats. It's super obvious."

"If it bothers you, you should tell him," I insisted. I tried to imagine myself in her position, and I had to admit that I'd probably like my mates being that possessive, but that didn't mean everyone wanted that.

"It doesn't." She deflated. "That's the problem. It's just confusing."

I considered what she was saying before nodding

in understanding. "I get that. Maybe you should tell them that they're confusing you?"

"Maybe..." She sighed and then offered me a tight smile. "If I'm confused, you must be going through a lot—realizing you're a dragon must be crazy."

"It was a lot." I exhaled. "I'm still not fully adjusted."

I wanted to tell her more about the situation, to show her that I trusted her as much as she trusted me, I just knew that right now was not the moment to do that. Especially because while the dining hall was somewhat empty, there were still people around.

"I have so many questions about that," Rachel admitted.

"Let's have a girls night and I can explain better then?" I suggested, looking around the room.

"Absolutely," she said, catching onto my meaning. "Which means it's probably time to work on this project."

"A 3D model of the universe, right?"

"Exactly. I love crafting, so I brought as many supplies as I could manage."

"They're so pretty," I said, examining all her craft supplies with interest. I had only ever been into knitting, but her supplies were so...sparkly. Markers. Stickers. Colored Paper. Glitter. I could easily see how fun it would be to create all different types of art with it.

"If you ever come over, back to my real house, I'll show you everything I have," she promised. "My mom and sisters love crafting too—we have a room for it."

That was so freakin' cool. I was tempted to ask her where she lived in Trabea and what clan territory it was in, but I figured that could wait.

* * *

It turned out that Rachel really did have everything we needed. Deciding to make a vertical structure for the model, we used wire to keep it upright and craft paper to represent the planes of existence. By the end of our craft session, we had created a fairly large structure, one that I hoped would impress our professor.

I offered Rachel an amused look.

"What?" she asked curiously.

"You know we're going to get a good grade, right?" I nudged her with my elbow, lowering my voice. "I mean, that's your freakin' mate."

Her cheeks pinkened again. "I'm pretending he's not for this project—for any of the classes he teaches for me." And I had absolutely no idea how she was doing that.

"Right..." I teased.

Suddenly, the sound of a chair clattering to the ground drew my attention to the far corner of the room. Immediately I was up, a flare of defensiveness and anger hitting me square in the chest.

"Where is it?" a tall, dark-haired woman demanded. She stood over a small male laid out on the floor, his eyes wide and breathing panicked. I couldn't tell what type of shifter he was, but at the concerned sound Rachel made, I had a feeling he was a prey animal. Or maybe it was the predatory energy coming off the woman that was scaring him.

To be fair, she was literally double both our heights.

"I have to work on it tonight—*ow!*"

The woman stepped right down on his hand, her combat boots crunching down on his fingers, and I found myself walking across the room before I could sort out why. The air grew charged as my mates entered the room, clearly realizing something was going on, and Rachel called my name hesitantly, concern coating her tone. I didn't turn back. I could see the malice radiating off this woman, and I could also tell she was enjoying hurting the guy. That she would continue to hurt him if someone didn't step in.

"You know what happens if you don't—"

"Stop."

My voice was far colder than I'd ever heard it before. The woman paused, her boot suspended in mid-air above the boy's chest as she looked up at me, giving him a split second to roll out of the way. Everyone around the woman looked extremely nervous, but I didn't feel that way at all. I felt angry at how she'd been treating him. Maybe it was better I'd been in the Bronzeheart estate for the past eight years, because if this was what shifter society was about, I wanted absolutely no part in it.

"Stop?" she demanded, appearing in front of me in a blink, causing me to freeze in surprise. "Who are you to tell me to stop? That little bastard owes me an assignment."

"I don't care," I whispered, examining her sharp face. Her skin was glinting with yellow scales underneath the pearly pale surface, her purple eyes narrowed into snake-like slits. "I don't care what he owes you, you don't need to hurt him. It's unnecessary."

"Unnecessary?!" She barked out a laugh, and before I could prepare for it, her hands shot out and she shoved me hard. I groaned, falling to the floor as the sudden shock and pain had tears pricking my eyes.

Breaker appeared at my side. "Bex—"

"I'm fine," I said loudly, sitting up and glancing at my mates. "Please let me handle this."

I wasn't positive why, but something instinctively told me it was important for me to handle this myself, to get her to understand that treating those she saw as weaker like this was total crap. I didn't watch their reactions as I stood up, my ears buzzing as anger flushed my face, the creature inside of me hyper-focused on the woman.

"Unnecessary? You want to see unnecessary?!" She grabbed a girl nearby, her shocked gasp filling the space, and threw her down at her feet. Everyone moved out of the way and stood up from their tables, looking fearful for the girl.

I was shaking now. I stepped forward, feeling a unique energy roll over my skin. I didn't want to shift —I knew that would be bad—but my vision was blurring, everything warping by the anger I felt at the injustice taking place.

"Leave. Her. Alone."

My voice was hard, and I could see the woman waver momentarily, her gaze solely on me. I don't think she recognized who I was or what was going on around us, that there were three other dragons in the room. Scales rippled down her body, like she was about to bust out of her own skin. I had no idea what type of shifter she was or how potentially dangerous she was to me; I didn't care because it didn't matter.

"Leave her alone?!"

"Don't!" I demanded as she bent down to grab the girl's neck. My voice seemed to vibrate through the room, and a spark of electricity crackled in the air near her. The woman looked at me with pure malice, but she didn't move. *Couldn't* move.

That infuriated her. She let out an enraged sound, and I shouldn't have been surprised when she launched herself at me—*except she never hit me.*

Instead she was thrown across the room into a set of tables. I looked towards my men, only to find them staring at me in surprise.

What in the fates had just happened? Better yet, why had *Diane* just hit this chick?

"Leave the dragon alone, Sue!" Diane barked. "Fuck off."

"Dragon?" Sue paled, her eyes widening on me while she stumbled to stand. "Fuck, that's why I was listening to you."

Then she was gone.

My brows went up in surprise, the anger draining out of me as I looked at Diane. "You...helped me."

"I did." Diane shrugged. "Don't think about it.

Didn't want to lose Sue to your psychotic mates—she's strong."

"They wouldn't hurt her," I promised, "but still, thank you."

Diane examined my gaze before looking towards my mates. "*Right.* Stay away from my people, Bexley."

Was it the time to remind her that *her* people were the ones causing the problems? I didn't want to sound mean, and this clearly wasn't Diane's fault... At least I didn't think it was.

Before I could decide what to say, she was gone, and I turned to find Rachel staring at me in surprise.

"What?" I asked, brows raised.

She nodded behind her, and when I turned around, the group of prey shifters were all staring at me in shock. The first guy, a freshman like myself, offered me a hesitant, almost nervous, smile. "Thank you s-so much. You didn't have to do that."

"Really," a second girl added, "that was so nice of you."

I frowned in confusion. "Of course I helped—she was hurting you."

All of them seemed surprised by my words and began to talk quietly amongst themselves. I turned back towards Rachel, and any tension, even from being near my mates, seemed gone as she offered me a warm smile.

"That was cool of you, Bexley. Seriously."

"It *was* cool of her," said a familiar voice that had my mates moving closer to me.

They didn't need to be protective or worried, though—it was Fletcher. The wolf shifter offered me a head nod in greeting before doing the same to my mates and then turning to Rachel. "And you, little bunny, need to get back to your dorm. It's almost evening."

"He calls her *little bunny*," I whispered to my mates. My friend shot me a scowl as her nose twitched.

"Right." She huffed and offered me a smile. "I'll see you in class tomorrow? I'll bring the project!"

"Absolutely," I said, waving at the two of them before turning towards my mates. "Well, that was successful. Don't know if you saw it, but the 3D model looks great."

"More successful than for just that reason," Jagger said. "The prey shifters over there are still talking about what you did."

"Does no one ever stand up for them?"

"Usually other shifters don't get involved," Breaker said apologetically. "I'll be the first to admit that we've ignored shit unless it's extremely, obviously wrong."

"Today would have been one of those times," Gage agreed. "It's different when shifters are similar in power levels, but when it's that off balance, it just turns messy."

"I just hope Sue, or whatever her name is, lays off." I shook my head. "I was surprised she listened to me."

"Dominance," Jagger explained. "She's a snake shifter—powerful, but nothing compared to a dragon."

"I see," I murmured in surprise. Not because of the dominance factor, but because I had to imagine that her shifted snake form was big. The thought sent a chill down my spine.

Gage chuckled as the other two offered me confused looks.

I shrugged before admitting, "I don't like snakes."

Chapter Ten

Jagger Silvershade

My little treasure was that and so much more—the woman was a fucking wonder.

Which was why I was staring at her like a lovesick idiot as we sat around the fire watching a vintage movie that was being projected on a nearby wall. Bexley's eyes lit up in humor as the human actress, Audrey something or another, said a joke that had the male actor laughing. Her smile grew as she continuously looped silver yarn back and forth in a graceful pattern I found mesmerizing to watch.

Then again, this moment in general was a bit surreal.

I had imagined so many elements of my future life with Bexley, but somehow sitting around the fire as she knitted and we talked lazily about the rugby game and her new classes, doing our best to avoid heavier topics, was becoming one of my favorites.

Still, while it felt natural, the fact that she had the ability to get the three of us to sit around and watch a movie like this on a Sunday night was a true miracle. I'm not positive what I would normally be doing—probably working, if I had to hazard a guess—but it wouldn't be something nearly as relaxing. Although *relaxing* was very much what we needed before this upcoming week.

If the Bronzehearts were serious, which I was positive they were, then my parents were about to get a heavy dose of reality served to them. Not that I minded. In fact, I was more than eager for the truth to be out there.

I had wanted to tell my parents, namely my mom, for a very long time now, that Bexley was still alive and very much my mate. Like I'd said, I had a feeling they knew. But in true Silvershade fashion, they tried to stay as un-opinionated about it as possible. Reservation to the extreme.

My parents were affectionate and kind individuals at their core, truly, but they were very different from the Bronzehearts or Firespells. They ruled their clan with a cold and calculating edge rather than through intimidation or power. It was why there had always been tension between the Silvershades and Firespells, with the Bronzehearts serving as a mediating force.

That didn't even include the part Bexley's family had played in all of this...

But yeah, despite hating that I had to go so long without seeing my little treasure, I was glad in some ways to know she had ended up with the Bronzehearts. Out of the three clan families, they had no doubt provided Bexley with the most 'normal' lifestyle.

My family would've been far too cold for Bexley's warmth. Then again, maybe they would have warmed up because of her. My mom had always loved her, even when she was a child. Maybe the Silvershade residence would've turned into a sunshine paradise. At least I hoped that was the case for the future.

I had no idea how we were going to split living between clan territories, unless we... Well, there was only one solution I could think of. The rogue lands were situated overlooking the rest of Trabea, and while not currently occupied by a ruling force, that hadn't always been the case.

For the longest time, it had been home to

Bexley's family. I still remember the first time I saw her estate...

"It's like a castle," I whispered loudly. My mom let out an amused hum, my father offering me a look over the newspaper he was reading before drawing his eyes to the estate and nodding in agreement.

I returned to looking at it, wishing they'd provided me with a bit more of a response. But as always, my parents were careful about their opinions. It was normal to me, but I heard people at our house, specifically the advisors, talking when they thought no one was listening about how it could be frustrating.

I was glad they somewhat agreed, though. It really did seem magical. The walls were made of a warm sunstone, and the tall towers and gardens were something out of a fairytale. I found myself liking it more than I'd expected.

I think part of why I liked it, though, was because I knew without a doubt that my friend Bex would be there.

It had only been two months since I'd met her, and since then we'd seen each other at one of the clan estates almost every other weekend, as well as having joint tutoring sessions during the week. While we were older than her, she was working on nearly the same level as we were. The official reason was something about combining resources to teach the future generation, but for me it just meant I could see Bexley twice a week.

Which was why I was so excited to see Bexley's home and stay there for the weekend. As we traveled up the mountainside and finally arrived at the large courtyard filled with guards and arriving guests, I caught sight of the Bronzeheart and Firespell family cars. Both parked and empty.

My friends were probably already inside, talking to Bexley. I wanted to be with them.

Getting out before the car came to a stop, despite my father's disapproving sound, I jogged towards the stairs of the estate.

"Jagger!" An explosion of red fabric appeared out of nowhere, and Bex launched herself towards me. Her hug was tight and my heart squeezed happily, glad my friend was thrilled to see me. I didn't look back to see how my parents reacted—I knew they didn't mind me being friends with Bex.

It was the one thing they'd made their opinion very clear on.

"Jagger." Breaker's voice pulled me from my thoughts. I'd been staring into the fireplace, feeling exhausted after everything that had happened this weekend. Despite landing a few good hits to the assholes that had distracted us from Ioan's attack on Bexley, I still felt frustrated and on edge.

I didn't like not knowing if they were an actual threat or not to Bexley's safety, and while I didn't think they had any information, there was always a chance. I was glad the Bronzehearts wanted to get everything out into the open. Then no one could ever claim they had something over her.

"Zoned out, sorry. What's up?" I sat up, looking around for Bex.

"She fell asleep. Gage just moved her," Breaker said. "Before that, though, he got a message from his parents—apparently they talked to the headmistress, and our plans to leave before the weekend may work out better than we expected."

"Really? Why?" I sat forward, putting my elbows on my knees.

"In the other sectors, there have been active security threats—I'm not sure where or how many, but I plan to find out. I don't like the idea of the academy being in danger and having that near Bex."

I nodded in agreement.

"But because of that," he continued, "there will probably be a meeting tomorrow morning. I don't think they will cancel class—shit, maybe they will if it's serious enough—but it would be a good excuse to leave without alerting any of the other students. We don't want extra attention on Bex until the formal announcement is made."

"Hopefully it works out that way, then," I murmured, standing. "I'm going to try to get some actual sleep tonight. Are you—"

"Finishing up a project for Professor Vin, and then I can sleep." Breaker shook his head, his frustration clear. "School has completely fallen to the wayside, to be honest."

I more than understood that. "Don't stay up too late," I said as I passed him, clapping him on the shoulder. When I walked into Bex's bedroom, I wasn't surprised to find Gage spread out on one side of her, completely passed out. His rugby games normally wore him out, and last night he hadn't gotten much sleep.

None of us had been getting a lot of sleep lately.

Although I had no idea why he wasn't sleeping well, especially after what I suspected happened between Bexley and him last night. If I came home smelling like Bexley's desire, I would sleep so fucking easily.

On second thought, I would probably be distracted as fuck with her scent surrounding me like that—even thinking about it turned me on.

Shaking myself from that thought before I got uncomfortably hard, I sat on the nearby chair, closing my eyes and sinking into it. I would have slept on the bed, but I had a feeling that I would just end up tossing and turning and keeping her up.

Ever since the Ioan thing, I hadn't been able to sleep deeply—at least not without the knowledge that one of us was up on watch. Since Gage needed the rest and Breaker was mostly focused on his schoolwork, I would do my best to assist in keeping watch. Closing my eyes, I turned my ears to everything going on outside of our dorm, the hum of the night relaxing.

I tried to stay alert, but the longer my eyes were closed, the more appealing sleep became...

"Jagger?" A familiar sing-song feminine voice was the next thing that graced my ears. I blinked my eyes open to the bright morning light, almost immediately knowing it was far later than I normally would've slept. But my attention wasn't truly on that. Instead, it was focused on Bexley sitting on the bed and staring at me with a sweet smile.

"Good morning!" she chirped. "Here's some coffee, sleepy head."

"I didn't mean to sleep," I admitted while taking the mug from her. I didn't want her to accidentally spill it on herself since the bed was bouncing and not super stable.

"I'm glad you did," she said.

"Wait—what time is it?" I asked curiously after taking a long sip, my voice rough from sleep.

"Almost time for you to walk me to class," she teased. My gaze ran over her, and I realized that she was already dressed for the day—although I hated to admit that, because what she was dressed in wasn't an outfit she should be able to wear out. She was so damn distracting.

Her long legs were covered in camel-colored suede that showed every inch of her curves, and a soft sweater covered her torso, drawing my eyes to her cleavage where a diamond pendant lay. Everything Bex wore made her look amazing, but some clothes made her look as soft to the touch as I knew she was. I loved that. I loved the idea of her being comfortable, and I knew she would be the most comfortable in my bed, naked.

Well, she would be more than fucking comfortable, but I wasn't going to let my mind go there. Not yet. Not this early in the day.

Putting down my coffee on the floor, I crooked my finger at her. She made a surprised noise but instantly crawled onto my lap. I groaned as my fingers ran over her ass and pulled her flush against my chest, loving how she rolled her hips naturally against my hard length while melting into my embrace.

I didn't hesitate to use one of my hands to grasp her chin and mold our lips together. When she let out a small moan, my cock jumped, loving how responsive she was. She poured every ounce of passion into everything she did, and right now it was kissing me and trying to be as close to me as fucking possible.

When I finally pulled back, needing a second to breathe before I pinned her to the bed, she stared at me with flushed cheeks and a beautiful smile that nearly had my heart thumping out of my chest.

"Jagger..." she whispered.

"I know." I pressed my forehead to hers, trying to steel myself. *I had to get her to class. I had to make sure she got to class.*

Suddenly, three shrill alarms blared, bringing my thoughts to a hard stop. There was only one reason for those alarms to be going off, and when the head-mistress's voice sounded through the room, seemingly out of nowhere, Bexley looked around frantically in confusion. I had a feeling what this was about; I just wished I'd had time to warn my mate, who looked suddenly very confused and concerned.

"Attention all students. Please make your way to

the pavilion for a mandatory emergency meeting. We expect you to all be prompt, and we will be gathering in thirty minutes. Professors will be at your gates to take attendance before you cross over, and if you are not listed on the roll, you will be immediately expelled from the academy. No exceptions."

Maybe I didn't *have to get her to class today.*

Chapter Eleven

Bexley

As we walked down the forested path towards the rest of the dorms, I felt a chill of apprehension roll over my skin. It was clear this type of thing wasn't the 'norm,' and while my mates didn't seem particularly worked up about it, I couldn't help but feel a level of tension.

I didn't know Headmistress Estrid well, but her tone of voice had been extremely serious in her announcement, and any desire I'd been feeling moments before had been washed away in an icy shower of concern.

"I promise it's not a big deal," Breaker assured.

"He's right," Jagger confirmed. "At least not for us. It's a security threat for some of the other sectors, but we can use it to get out of here and go back to the Bronzeheart estate."

Gage made a sound of agreement. "I already let my parents know we'd be leaving this afternoon."

"Wait—" I paused on the path and examined their expressions. "How do you know all this? Did your parents call the school like they'd mentioned?"

"Yes," Gage answered, "but more than that, we're usually fed important information like this about the rest of the school, not only for our security but now yours. I don't care if it's a different sector, it has the potential to affect you."

"Which means we need to know," Breaker finished. I felt a small blush invade my cheeks at the serious nature of their statement and protective intensity of their expressions.

"Alright." I drew my lip in. "I want to know what's going on also—so feel free to tell me." Gage nodded and Jagger squeezed my hand in agreement as we stepped into the central courtyard of our sector, the space filled to the brim with students.

All at once I felt a wave of overwhelming power from so many shifters being in a confined area. It wasn't a power or dominance thing, it was just a lot of magic and a lot of different scents. I was starting to realize that since shifting, my senses had changed, expanded and opened up to the world around me in a way that could be overwhelming.

That sensation wasn't helped by the fact that

people almost immediately began staring at us and talking in low murmurs.

I kept my hand in Jagger's as Gage walked in front of me and Breaker followed behind, their energy encasing me in a protective cocoon of magic. I looked through the crowd for familiar faces as people let us pass to the front of the sector near the gate. I didn't see Rachel, but as we reached the exit, I found Diane surrounded by a group of individuals glaring at me. Her attention was on Fletcher across from her, her brow arched and an amused expression on her face.

"Fletcher. Diane," I greeted both of them, studying the gate of the sector which was currently manned by a professor I didn't recognize. Clearly they weren't letting anyone through just yet though.

"Bexley." Fletcher offered a short greeting, looking more tense than usual

"Bex." Diane smirked, looking away from Fletcher. "See, wolf boy? I knew the dragons would get here. Now we don't have to fight over who walks through first."

"Wait, what?" I asked Jagger.

"They were fighting about which group was going to go through the gate first. We outrank both of them in dominance, so now it's not a problem," Jagger explained.

"Fates," I murmured, shaking my head and looking at the two groups in mild frustration. "Why is everything an argument with shifters?"

Breaker let out a deep chuckle that drew surprised and confused expressions from those around us, as if they had never heard him laugh before. I loved the sound of it, and when I looked up at my mates, I found them staring at me in amusement, as if what I said was funny.

Fletcher grunted and admitted, "She's not wrong."

"I'm a pacifist, you're the problem." Diane shrugged.

"Right..." Sue appeared from the back of the group, offering Diane an amused look. "Same."

"I don't think you're a pacifist," I contradicted in a soft murmur, causing Sue to glare at me. But after only a moment she looked away, clearly not wanting to push it.

"Professor Vin, can we get through?" Breaker called out.

"Soon," he said dismissively, looking back down at his clipboard. I examined the wolves Fletcher was surrounded by, looking for one specific person.

"Wait—Fletcher, where is Rachel?"

His eyes darkened, and the wolves around him went quiet. I got the feeling that I'd brought up something I wasn't supposed to. I didn't back down though.

"No idea." He shrugged and I frowned, stepping forward slightly.

"Is she with your—"

"No idea," he said a bit harder this time, causing Gage to let out a rumble in warning.

In that moment I completely understood why Rachel felt insecure about her place with Fletcher. It was obvious that he was trying to keep their connection quiet, at least around other wolves, *but why?* I didn't think it wasn't that he didn't care about her. In fact, I knew he did. A flare of annoyance hit me in the chest in defense of my friend.

Pain flashed across his face, so fast I would've missed it if I'd blinked, so I finished the conversation with a simple statement. "Don't hurt her, Fletcher."

I hadn't meant it as a demand, but the power behind my words had him straightening and narrowing his eyes at me. Jagger's hand tightened on my waist, and Diane let out a low whistle but otherwise stayed quiet. Instead of arguing, though, Fletcher just offered a sharp nod and looked away as the gates opened up.

"One by one," Professor Vin called out. Gage led me forward, cutting off the conversation.

Crap. I frowned slightly as Professor Vin

checked off my name, my thoughts straying to what I'd just done. Had I used my magic? My dominance? Like with Sue? I didn't want to do that to a friend, but I also didn't regret telling him how I felt. I liked Fletcher, but if he hurt Rachel...

"You did nothing wrong," Jagger assured me as we stepped through the gate, out of the sector and into the pavilion where we had originally portalled in.

"He shouldn't be hiding his mate," Breaker agreed.

Before I had a chance to respond to him, we were being ushered towards a certain section of the pavilion. It was clear that the professors and academy were doing their best to keep all six sectors separate, teachers lining the borders and paths so we couldn't interact. It was a shame because I couldn't help but look around in interest, my gaze catching some of the other students before Jagger's defensive rumble had them looking away. Specifically the males.

"Stay here, and don't talk to anyone else," a secondary professor instructed as we stood at the head of our group, facing the main academic building. I noticed that unlike the other sector groups, which seemed haphazardly organized, the shifter sector was aligning itself naturally with dominance and hierarchy.

"Why can't we talk to anyone else?" I asked, looking up at my mates. The three of them always seemed large to me, but as they talked in quiet tones to one another, literally looking over everyone, they seemed larger than life. Their gazes were on all the other sectors, and I honestly didn't blame them. It was fascinating being around so many different types of creatures.

Demigods. Fae. Demons. Vampires. Witches. The power influx around us was intoxicating, and I couldn't help but just breathe it in for a moment. Well, until someone appeared next to me.

"It turns out I didn't have to go to your sector to ask for the 'shifter who doesn't shift.'" The familiar feminine voice had me immediately smiling at my vampire friend, Alina. She stood on the edge of our sector, clearly not caring about the instructions to not talk to one another. As always, she looked impeccable and deadly, something I was positive my mates noticed as they drew closer behind me, a defensive energy rolling off of them.

"And I didn't have to go ask for the crazy..." I drew out the end with a small smile, not wanting to call her a bitch.

She chuckled softly, blue eyes sparking with amusement as she sensed my dilemma. "Bitch. Crazy bitch," she finished for me.

"I bet no one thinks that about you," I said honestly.

She huffed out a breath before shrugging her slender shoulders, "They might not say it out loud anymore because of who I'm associated with, but I've not done the best job at making friends in my sector."

Before I could ask who exactly she was associated with, she switched the topic. Her eyes flicked up and behind me, presumably at my mates, and she arched a brow. "Is this your security team or something?"

"My mates." I looked up to find all three of them hovering like I had sort of expected and hoped for. Not because I was worried about Alina, but because I liked them near me.

"This is Alina," I said. "She's my friend from the vampire sector. Alina, these are my mates, Gage, Jagger, and Breaker."

"Three mates," she murmured and offered me a small smirk before her head swiveled to glance at the two vampires at the front of her group. One was easily distinguishable as a professor from the way he carried power and surveyed the students, but the other had his back to us. "Seems we have even more in common now, Bex."

My cheeks flushed red as I stumbled over my words. "Do you have..." I paused, wondering if it was rude to ask if she meant she also had multiple mates. Unsure, I went in a different direction. "I just shifted recently and realized I'm a—"

"Dragon?" she hazarded a guess and then tilted her head in thought. "Honestly, I really assumed you would've been something less—"

"Deadly," I finished for her.

An authentic smile flashed on her face, show-casing her fangs. "Yes that," she agreed, before her gaze shaded darker. "Although with everything going on in this academy, being deadly works in your favor."

"I feel like I'm out of the loop," I admitted. "I didn't realize there was even a reason to have a meeting."

"I heard the witch sector may be having prob-lems," Jagger said in a quiet tone. Both Alina's and my gazes darted over to where the witch sector stood, and I perked up slightly, seeing a familiar face at the front.

The woman standing there was the one I'd met. Deva.

"You know her?" Alina asked, a curious note to her voice.

"We met on the way to the party. I think my mates know her men," I said, nodding towards the five shadows that surrounded her, darkness emanating off of them like a warning beacon. Deva had this otherworldly glow to her, like she wasn't exactly real. It wasn't like the other witches around her—she was something different for sure.

"Well, you know how to pick friends." Alina smirked. "Good thing you have the three bodyguards for mates."

I arched a brow in confusion, and her eyes softened in understanding.

"I know 'dangerous' when I see it, and that woman in the witch sector is exactly that. Between your choice of friends and mates, you seem to surround yourself with dangerous people is what I'm saying," she translated.

"Dangerous?" I titled my head up at my mates and smirked. "I mean, their dragons are dangerous, but they're pretty sweet."

Just then our attention was drawn to Estrid, who'd suddenly exited the academic building. I leaned back against Gage as my other two mates drew closer.

As Estrid stepped onto a raised platform, her gaze meeting each of the professors' that stood at the front of the sector groups, an uneasy feeling washed over me.

She nodded to herself before beginning. "Thank you for coming, students. I know this is not how any of us wanted to spend our Monday morning, but we would be remiss in keeping you in the dark of what is going on at the academy. Recently, we've had several security breaches across multiple sectors."

Air whooshed out of me because her words were so much more concerning than what the boys had even suggested. Multiple? Security breaches? As in external threats? That was what that meant, right?

Gasps and hushed whispers filled the air, multiplying louder and louder until the space felt chaotic. I stepped back so that I was securely in between my mates, not liking the energy moving through the crowd. Clearly, Estrid felt very much the same.

"Silence!" Her hard demand had everyone freezing, her blazing blue eyes glowing with determination and a flare of dominance that I think had every shifter—including us—going silent.

"I know this is alarming—it's the first time our academy has ever faced a security breach, let alone multiple. Please know that all of the staff are working relentlessly to ensure your safety, and we will not rest until we can without a doubt say there is no longer a threat."

There was an eerie chill to her tone that had me knowing this was so much worse than she was even letting on. My nails dug into my palms as my hearing went static, nearly making me miss her explanation of the academy's plans on how to move forward from here. The part that stood out to me the most was about students who potentially wanted to leave and go home without consequences for the following year.

Well...I didn't want to leave DIA for the year, but my mates were right—it would work for the moment to get us off campus. Would classes be canceled then? I had to assume so. Although maybe not, because then what about everyone who wanted to stay?

I was so trapped in my thoughts that I hadn't realized the meeting was coming to a close until Alina spoke up, drawing my attention. There was concern in her gaze, her normal cool aloofness lessened. "Be careful, Bexley. I don't know what all is happening at DIA, but it isn't good. Stay safe."

Then, like at the night of the party, she was gone. I stared into the crowd she had slipped into and then turned back to my mates. All of them looked relatively unconcerned, but the tension in their frames as we walked through the crowd back towards the gate of our sector told a much different story.

It wasn't until we'd walked through the gate of our sector that I realized everyone was gathered in front of the main academic building, Professor Clanguard standing with the other professors at the top of the stone steps.

Rachel stood next to him, offering me a small, cheery wave. *Oh, that's where she was!* Clearly, Professor Clanguard didn't plan on keeping their relationship a secret anymore. I couldn't help but smile at how happy she looked, and when I searched the crowd for Fletcher, he was nowhere in sight.

"Listen up!" Professor Clanguard spoke loud enough to draw everyone's attention. "Classes will be canceled for the next two to three days. You will be notified when they resume. While we haven't had any incidents within our sector, we will be enhancing security so that you can feel as comfortable as possible. Everyone understand?"

Murmured sounds of agreement and nods followed, and when another professor dismissed everyone, I turned to find my mates all seeming to have a silent conversation.

"Hey." I rolled up on my toes and let out a small frustrated noise, drawing their attention. "If you're going to have super secret silent conversations, please *include* me."

Jagger's gaze moved down to me, a bit of humor there. "Sorry, little treasure. We were just thinking it'd be better to leave now than later—I'm not sure what it will be like with new security here, and I'd rather not delay us leaving."

"Well that sounds reasonable. Let's go then."

"Just like that?" Breaker smirked.

"I'm excited to go home," I said, bouncing on my toes. "Especially because it means eating Ms. Payne's cupcakes—I *will* be bringing some of those back with me to school."

Chapter Twelve

Bexley

"I'm pretty much ready to go," I said while accounting for everything that I planned to pack in my small weekend bag. I still had plenty of items back at the Bronzeheart estate, so I wasn't that worried about forgetting something.

Still, there were a few essentials that I always had on me, including my stuffed dragons which were currently finding a home inside the backpack that Breaker had on his lap.

I had no idea how I was pulling it off—or maybe I wasn't—but I was trying my best to not sound shaken about the meeting earlier. More than anything, though, I felt worried about everyone at the academy and the security breaches she had mentioned. As I thought back on the meeting and the fear I saw in some of the passing faces, I couldn't help but face the reality that there was something scary happening here. The creature inside of me felt protective and defensive, not liking that there was a potential threat to a place we now considered home. It was unacceptable.

Trying to put it from my mind, though, was harder than I'd like to admit.

"*Mo chuisle*."

"Love that nickname," I admitted, offering him a soft, affectionate look.

"You seem worried." His brow dipped as he leaned forward, his massive frame filling my bedroom perfectly. I loved when my mates were in smaller spaces like this. I liked feeling like they were everywhere at once.

"I'm okay." I exhaled and tried to explain. "I'm just a bit thrown off by how freaked out everyone seemed to be—it makes me feel on edge. Also, I was excited about my new classes this week, and now at least half the week is canceled, which is a bit of a bummer."

"I promise we will be back as soon as this event is over. I prefer it here than back at any of our homes." Breaker took my hand and pulled me to stand between his legs. I put my hand on his large shoulders as he examined my expression and spoke honestly. "Although if we had a home, I would want to be there."

"I love the sound of that." I flushed, drawing my lip in. "I didn't even consider that. With all four of us being mates...how will that work?"

"I'm not sure, but we'll figure it out—we always do," Breaker assured me. I knew he was right. We would figure it out, and while it was a bit unexpected, I was excited to go back home and hear what Celine had to tell me about my family. It was like a missing puzzle piece dangling in front of me, and I was beyond eager to grab it.

"Let's head out!" Gage called from the other room. Breaker had already packed his own backpack, which he slung over his shoulders before helping me slide my own over my arms and onto my back. As I stepped back and tried to grab my weekend bag, he swooped in and took it, lifting it over his shoulder and offering me an affectionate knowing smile.

Not only did Breaker like picking me up, but he always insisted on carrying stuff for me. I found it super sweet but put a playful scowl on my lips just to remind him that I could carry the bag on my own if he'd let me.

Appearing in the door, I noticed that both men had small, dark bags like Breaker, and I started to wonder if my weekend bag was overdoing it.

"That's all you're bringing? That doesn't seem like enough." Jagger said, contradicting my thoughts.

"Oh, just wait until you see what she has back at the house." Gage smirked, causing my cheeks to turn bright pink. I'd never really thought of my space at home as over the top, but now that he mentioned it, I felt the need to warn my other two mates.

"Okay, so that isn't entirely my fault," I said, putting my hands on my hips. "Celine loves shopping for me! And I told Gage once that I loved the sparkly car he gave me, and then he convinced me to redo the entire bathroom like that!"

Gage barked out a laugh. "Right, a ton of convincing that took."

"Yeah, I'm never feeling guilty about those damn notes again." Breaker chuckled, causing my chest to squeeze with affection at the reminder. I was glad he had said it out loud. I didn't think he was hiding it from the others, but it did feel nice to be able to talk about it now.

"Nor the flowers," Jagger murmured.

My head snapped his way. "Flowers?"

"Yeah, what flowers?" Gage asked in mock confusion.

"Yeah..." The tips of Jagger's ears turned red as he ran a hand through his hair, clearly not having meant to say it out loud. "The flowers you received every day were from me."

Fates, this man was going to kill me. He was so freakin' sweet.

Approaching him, I grabbed his hand and tilted my head back to examine his slightly embarrassed expression. "Wait, really? I absolutely loved those. Seriously, it was one of my favorite parts of the day."

"Well now I'm jealous," Gage muttered, causing Jagger to flash a smile, any hesitancy disappearing with my words. Despite the situation at hand, I had to admit there was a lightness to these three men that hadn't been around before everything came to light. I just hoped that this event and bringing the truth to light to the public wouldn't put more stress on them.

"Shit," Jagger cursed, looking down at his expensive, shiny watch. "If we're going to get through the portal now, we need to go."

That set us all into action. I knew we would be back in no time, but as we took the elevator down, I couldn't help but look over my dorm one last time.

This place had become home so fast, and I knew it was because of my mates.

"She is so nice—I hate to see her so tense and worried," I whispered in the darkness of the car as Headmistress Estrid passed back through the portal and disappeared out of sight. The hill and wooden arch were just as I remembered them, but unlike the lighthearted and relaxed air that Estrid had exhibited that first time, she'd seemed unusually quiet today. She hadn't commented on the four of us going back home, instead simply telling us to be safe. Her mind had seemed a million miles away, and I couldn't help but worry about her, remembering the darkness in her gaze as she'd walked back through the portal.

"You are too damn sweet for this world, little treasure," Jagger rumbled out from next to me. The skies outside were gloomy, and while Gage talked to the driver outside of the car, the three of us buckled up and settled in for the drive to the Bronzeheart estate.

"What do you mean?" I asked in confusion.

"You are more empathetic than anyone I know," Jagger explained. "It's fucking beautiful, but sometimes people aren't deserving of your empathy. I'm not talking about Headmistress Estrid, of course, but there are others who would try to take advantage of you."

"Which is why it's good to have us around,"

Breaker said, offering me a flash of a smile. "See, Bexley? We are useful."

"You're more than just useful," I said happily. "You're my mates."

Jagger let out a rumble of agreement, and Breaker's gaze flashed with heat. Before they could say anything in response, the door opened and Gage slipped in. "We're good to go. The estate is under preparations for the event tomorrow evening, but neither of your families have arrived yet. Apparently they'll be staying the night tomorrow, though."

"Wonderful." Breaker exhaled. Suddenly, my relaxed anchor of a mate was on edge. Deciding I didn't want to hold back, I unbuckled and slipped across the way, wrapping my arms around his neck and cozying up on his lap. Almost immediately he relaxed, and I felt far better knowing I could help him, even a little bit.

I didn't know about his relationship with his parents, but I had a feeling it was more tense than Jagger's relationship with his, and for sure more tense than Gage's family. I honestly couldn't tell you if I had ever seen Celine and Leopold argue. I'm sure they had—I knew they'd debated a lot of different topics over the years, but none of it was combative or angry, just a difference of opinion.

I felt like I was going in blind when it came to all

these other relationships, and I hoped that my memories would begin to return far faster than they had been.

Small things had already started to trickle through, like how I used to love lemonade. It was such an odd memory to have, but I distinctly remember drinking it almost every day during the summer. So much so that our kitchen staff would have it brought to me without asking.

But as much as I loved small tidbits like that, they didn't truly help with our larger problem.

"*Mo chuisle*, we're here."

My eyes opened, making me realize I had momentarily dozed off, and I let out a small yawn. Breaker helped me out of the car, and I noticed that the other two had walked ahead towards the main entrance of the house, probably because they hadn't wanted to wake me up.

"Where are they going?" I asked as staff members began to take our bags into the estate. Instead of going through the main entrance, though, Breaker led me towards the side and down a path that led towards the gardens. I was still wearing my outfit from before, the camel-colored pants and sweater, but I had to admit it was a bit chillier than I would have expected, so the way Breaker was holding me close to him so I would stay warm was much appreciated.

"The Bronzehearts are in a meeting—phone call with Jagger's parents, according to Mr. Webb—I figured we could go to your room, especially since you're tired."

"I like the sound of that." I nodded towards the breezeway on the left side of the garden that led to the annex of the house where I stayed.

Breaker let out a low rumble. "Oh, I know where your bedroom is."

"You do?" I tilted my head, finding that both really interesting and attractive. My center tightened as I wondered if he ever tried to look in on me. I mean...he'd been leaving notes at least once a week. It wouldn't be out of the realm of possibility.

"You have no idea how many times I thought about walking right in here," he said as he led me through the large doors of my bedroom and into the luxurious living space, the familiar scent instantly making me feel at home. "I wanted to tell you everything in those notes, but I was worried if I started to say too much..."

"You would never stop," I whispered, turning into him. He cupped my jaw, examining my face with heat and affection. The mix had me feeling dizzy, and my gaze darted down to his lips.

"Exactly," he drew out. "I would never fucking stop."

Rolling up on my toes, I tried to meet his lips, wanting to feel that connection to him, and without a second thought he swept me off my feet so that I was wrapped around him. His hands ran over my butt as I locked my ankles around his waist, and my hands slid into his hair. A soft moan of his name left my lips as he pressed me gently against one of the walls nearby, sliding his tongue against my lips and causing my entire body to shudder.

"Breaker," I whispered as he moved his lips down my jaw, the touch searingly hot as he reached the column of my throat. I let out a hiss as he drew in the skin there and sucked hard, the action causing my clit to pulse as my eyes nearly rolled back in my head. My nipples hardened against my bra, the moment of pleasure releasing a floodgate of need.

"Damnit," he groaned softly. "You have no idea how much I want to mark you, how much I want to see you wearing my bite on your pretty little neck, *mo chuisle*."

"Please do that again," I whispered, my voice nearly a plea. "Please, Breaker?"

"*Fuck*, you never have to beg me," he growled, searing his lips to mine before hoisting me further up on the wall so his lips could move down my throat to my cleavage. I whimpered as he pushed up my sweater to reveal my lace bra. "But I have a better idea."

Pulling down the lace with his teeth, one hand cupped my breast as his thumb rolled over my nipple. A moan left my lips as I tightened my legs around him, my center pulsing with need, and I knew I was absolutely soaked. The sensation of him toying with me, only playing with my breast, was going to be enough to send me over the edge—

His teeth grazed my other breast, and everything inside of me convulsed.

"Holy fates—" I choked out as his hot mouth closed around my nipple, teasing it with his tongue. My thighs shook as I whimpered.

"Fuck," he rasped, breaking away for just a moment. "I can feel how needy you are, how much you need to come. Don't worry, *mo chuisle,* I won't make you suffer."

Before I could even process what he was saying, his teeth tugged on my nipple and everything around me went black before exploding in an inferno of pleasure. My hands tightened in his hair as I cried out his name, climaxing from him teasing my breasts alone. Breaker let out a groan as he ground against me, his cock seeming to only get harder at the sound of my orgasm.

My entire body sagged in relief, the frustration that always seemed to simmer under my skin, always ready to break out around my mates, sated. *Holy fates.*

"Like I said," Breaker murmured, his lips against my throat now. "I'll never fucking stop."

As he pulled back, adjusting my top, I kissed him hard and spoke against his lips. "I don't want you to stop—ever."

"I hope you mean that, Bex, because I'm not going anywhere."

I more than meant it, I just had to figure out how to show him I meant it.

Chapter Thirteen

Bexley

"This can *not* be considered a good breakfast."

"Oh, hush. The girl needs more food. Fates, you know they aren't feeding her enough at that academy. If she wants a cupcake, then she gets ten," Ms. Payne scolded Mr. Webb, who was staring at the plate of cupcakes in front of me. I let out a sound of agreement.

"Mr. Webb, you wouldn't believe it—the cupcakes they have there...they're glitter-less," I whispered in mock horror.

His eyes filled with amusement as he let out a long sigh. "Quite the travesty. You're right, Ms. Bexley, my apologies," he amended, causing me to let out a small giggle. It was hard to not be in a good mood though. As far as mornings went, this one was pretty darn perfect.

Not only was I sitting in my favorite kitchen, eating my third cupcake of the morning paired with peppermint coffee, but Mr. Webb and Ms. Payne were here! The familiarity and 'normal-ness' of the situation was causing me to feel settled and comfortable. It was exactly what I needed with everything going on.

The only downside to this morning was that I hadn't woken up next to my mates. While it was a recent thing, sleeping in the same bed as them, I had already gotten used to it, and I didn't want it to stop anytime soon. Although, the reason they weren't sleeping in my room was pretty freakin' funny, if you asked me.

Leopold and Celine had decided that despite being mates, it wasn't appropriate for them to sleep in my quarters—that is, until we were officially engaged or married. And since we hadn't even publicly announced that we were mates yet, they had to stay in Gage's suite or the guest rooms. It was a bit old-fashioned, especially since Gage had fallen asleep in my room before, but the way Celine's eyes lit up while announcing the stipulation about engagement or marriage told me that she was doing her best to speed up the 'timeline,' in her mind.

I wasn't sure what I thought about the engagement or marriage aspect. I mean, I did... I *totally* knew how I felt about it, but what was holding me back from committing fully was that I couldn't read my mates' feelings on it. They didn't seem surprised by her declaration—if anything, they'd seemed amused—but their lack of reaction to marriage being brought up a second time led me to believe that they'd either already assumed that would happen or they were just ignoring it.

My mates weren't exactly the type to ignore important things, I was learning.

And while I missed sleeping next to them, I did have to admit that having a bit of alone time wasn't the worst thing in the world. After the amazing orgasm Breaker had given me—one that I was still reeling from—I'd soaked in the tub for nearly two hours before doing a little spa night and falling asleep while my mates watched a game in the other room. I hadn't meant to fall asleep, but when I'd woken up alone around eleven at night, I'd stumbled sleepily towards the kitchen, my stomach rumbling and very clearly upset that we hadn't eaten dinner.

My lips pressed up, thinking about what I'd found in the kitchen.

. . .

"Have a nice nap, sleepy head?" Celine asked, eating out of a tub of ice cream. Leopold stood nearby eating some pasta, and I loved how the two of them were the picture of a normal couple. I let out a small yawn before going to the stove and taking a bowl of pasta from the food that was being reheated, my stomach growling loudly.

"I remember how hungry I was as a young shifter," Celine said, offering me a look of understanding.

"Same. I used to wake up at least four times throughout the night needing to eat," Leopold said. *"Rather distracting when you're in class."*

"I almost never miss meals," I admitted, taking a bite of pasta and sighing happily. *"My stomach gets very angry when I do."*

"You must have been tired to fall asleep without dinner," Celine said with concern.

"I haven't been sleeping very deeply—I actually haven't dreamed either." I frowned. *"It feels like my brain is fighting against it. I think it may have to do with the memory thing."*

"Is that the only reason you haven't been sleeping well? We may have some medicine or something if we talk to our physician," Leopold suggested.

"It's not the only reason, the adjustment to school is just hard," I lamented.

"Making friends?" Celine asked hopefully.

"Yes." I nodded. "Rachel—she's a bunny shifter."

"Prey shifter. Interesting," Leopold commented.

"Yeah, I didn't realize how mean everyone is to each other. It's like everything is a freakin' fight," I murmured. "All because of dominance. Like, why is it a big deal if I want to be partners with a bunny shifter?"

Celine let out a hum of understanding. "It's not a big deal for you, and it never will be. You're at the top of the food chain, and your dragon knows it. I suspect you've always known it in some way, even when it was being blocked, and because of that you don't have a need to fight for that dominance position—because you already hold it."

"But you may get challenges," Leopold admitted.

"I've heard," I huffed. "This girl Sue was threatening some prey shifters, and I made her stop. I thought she was going to challenge me for sure, but then she just stopped when I ordered her to."

Celine and Leopold stared at me in surprise before the first asked, "What type of shifter?"

"Snake."

"Strong." Leopold arched a brow at his wife. "To think she isn't even using an ounce of her power yet."

"Wait, what?" I looked between them.

Celine squeezed my hand. "You probably don't

see it yet, but you are so incredibly powerful, Bexley. I can't wait to see you fully embrace it."

I was still mulling over the words, both loving and hating them. Loving because knowing they believed in me so much made me feel a surge of self-confidence. I only hated it because I worried I wouldn't live up to that expectation, that I wouldn't be that powerful or that I would somehow disappoint them.

Taking another bite of my cupcake, I forced my thoughts back onto breakfast and lighter topics. *I wouldn't allow myself to think that way.*

"Another?" Ms. Payne offered the plate.

"Actually, I'm going to go find Mrs. Bronzeheart," I said. "If the guys come down here—"

"We'll tell them you're in the ballroom, dear." Ms. Payne offered me an understanding smile. "You'll find Mrs. Bronzeheart there."

"Thanks." Taking my mug with me as I walked out the room, I tried to not laugh at the sound of her scolding Mr. Webb for trying to eat my cupcakes. *This.* I had missed this.

I had also missed walking through these large marble halls in my pink fuzzy slippers. I was dressed in a pair of leggings and an oversized purple sweater that was super comfortable. Normally I would've tried to put on real clothes, but considering it was chilly this morning, this felt perfect. Plus, while I loved the marble, it could be cold on bare feet.

Despite the formal and grand nature of the Bronzeheart estate, it had always felt homey to me. I wouldn't say it was cozy, but there were parts to it that were, like the writing room that Celine used as her office, or the den on the first floor that we used as a family room. The ballroom, however, was not one of those places.

Reaching the three-story set of gold doors, I entered the ballroom. It was placed on an annex that jetted off the right side of the house, meaning that all the walls except for the one connected to the estate were made of floor-to-ceiling windows, allowing in as much light as possible to highlight the gilded ceiling and marble floors. It was a beautiful space, and my mouth opened slightly in surprise as I walked into a whirlwind of activity.

There were twenty or so staff members in the room, and so many boxes, bins, carts, and tables set up. I couldn't get a mental image of what they were trying to do, but it was clear that they were going all out. The french doors that led out to a grand garden in the back were open, allowing for people to move in and out as they brought in items from the trucks in the driveway. Excitement filled my chest, and I fought the urge to ask them about their vision for the space. I didn't want to get in anyone's way.

"Bex!" Celine appeared seemingly out of nowhere, spinning her way out of the sea of decorations. Her eyes were filled with sparkling excitement, and she was dressed in a mauve dress and heels, looking immaculate as usual.

"Hey! I came to chat, but I see that you're super busy—"

"Never busy when it comes to you," she promised, hooking arms with me. "I have information for you, anyway. Things that are important to know before tonight."

I sighed happily, glad she seemed on the same page as me, as she led me down the hall and towards her writing room. The sage green and gray color scheme had me taking a deep breath as I sat down on one of the green velvet couches, the doors closing behind us and leaving us in a comfortable silence. The fireplace was lit and crackling, pushing away any of the chill that had invaded the house.

"Tonight is going to be perfect," Celine said, grabbing something from her desk and coming to sit down next to me. "I don't want you to worry about anything. I promise that any concerns you have are not needed. While you may not remember many of the guests tonight, they will all remember you and be *thrilled* and relieved to know you've been safe all these years."

I breathed out, sinking into the couch. "They won't be mad?"

"No," she insisted. "While initially there was mistrust that caused a fight, over the years it dissolved, and now the divide only exists because of pride. Because people don't want to admit they were wrong to suspect one another. A mistake that cost us finding out who truly hurt your family. It didn't help that their loss hit everyone particularly hard."

"Why?" I asked softly.

An affectionate warmth filled her gaze. "Jericho and Ashley were loved by everyone. Every single person in Trabea loved them, even those that weren't from their clan. It didn't matter; everyone flocked to them naturally. They had this aura that people couldn't ignore. Something they passed down to you."

She said that so matter-of-factly, but I was far more caught up on the names.

"Jericho and Ashley are my parents' names?" I asked, my voice filled with emotion.

Sadness filled Celine's gaze as she squeezed my hand. "I know this must be so hard for you, not having your memories, but let me assure you of something. You were loved by them. You have always been loved, by your parents and by all the clans, from the moment you were born. It was why I didn't hesitate to bring you into our home. I will always consider you my daughter, but I never want to replace a mother that I know loved you with every ounce of her being, that only wanted, more than anything, for you to be safe and happy. When you get your memories back, you'll see that."

Tears filled my eyes and leaked down my face, causing me to try to blink them away. "I don't know how I'll feel about them when I get my memories back. I'm not sure what emotions will be attached with it, but you've shown me a level of love and acceptance I didn't think I deserved for the longest time."

Hugging me tightly, she spoke fiercely. "You deserve that and so much more. I think you'll see tonight just how much everyone mourned your loss."

It was so insane to think that an entire group of people had thought I'd died when I'd been living with the Bronzehearts this entire time. After savoring her hug for a long moment, I finally sat back and took a long sip of my coffee. I sifted through the stream of questions in my head, exhaling. "You said people loved my parents—did you? Were you friends?"

"Yes." Celine nodded enthusiastically. "Ashley and I were extremely close. She was the one who introduced me to Leopold, actually. We were from the same clan territory—the Flash Clan—the one your father's family ruled over. Here we were, two girls from a farming village, and this prince essentially shows up one day and just takes her! Kidnapped her! I was convinced I'd lost her, especially when he started courting her and talking about marriage, but instead she brought me into her new life, and the day of their wedding, when the other clans came to the celebration, I met Leopold."

"That's really sweet, both aspects," I whispered, loving that it hadn't been an arranged marriage. I wasn't positive if my parents had still been in love when they were taken from this life, but it sounded like they had been.

"I have so many stories." Celine sighed happily. "And for the longest time, I've wanted to take you back to where you grew up, to jog your memories, but we never wanted to cause you any unnecessary pain."

"You said my family's clan was the Flash Clan?" I asked curiously. "Where did I grow up, exactly? I have never even heard of a fourth clan."

"Purposefully," she admitted. "They're considered the rogue lands now."

"*That's* what Jagger meant about none of the clans claiming territory," I whispered.

"Which is why we think the attack was made for some other reason." She frowned. "Eight years, and we still have no idea what the hell happened."

"I'm going to remember, no matter what," I said fiercely. No matter what happened in my future, I had a family and mates I wanted to protect, and if there was an unknown force coming after me once I revealed I was alive... Well, I wanted to be as prepared as possible.

Suddenly, a knock sounded on the door, and Ms. Payne peeked her head in. "Ladies, just wanted to let you know that the seamstress is here for fittings."

"Oh good! Bring her here," Celine instructed, and Ms. Payne disappeared once again.

"I know we're getting short on time," Celine said, returning her focus to me before grabbing a book from the coffee table. "So I want to give you this. I've been putting it together these past few years—it has everything I know and can remember about your family, as well as any pictures I could hunt down."

"Thank you," I whispered as I put the gold leather book in my lap, my fingers running over the cold metal of the name embossed on the front cover.

Blackforge.

"Is this..."

"Your last name," Celine confirmed.

Bexley Blackforge.

Chapter Fourteen

Breaker Firespell

"It's only a matter of time until they show up."

Jagger walked out onto the stone balcony, exiting the large living suite where Bexley was having her makeup and hair done for tonight. I knew she was worried we were bored as we watched her get ready, but I was more than enjoying myself—especially after a night away from her. Don't get me wrong, I respected the Bronzehearts enough to listen to them, but I still didn't have to like that shit.

Waking up to her was my favorite way to start the day.

Silently acknowledging Jagger's statement, I turned to look at the driveway, waiting for the sight of my parents' car barreling this way. They'd already attempted to call me four times now, and every single one had gone unanswered. They'd figure out everything they needed to know soon enough.

There were far more important things to focus on, like watching the way Bexley laughed at something the woman doing her hair said. The sunlight hit my mate, making it appear like she was truly sparkling, and my chest constricted. How was it possible that such a beautiful woman existed in the first place? How was she real?

Normally I would hate the idea of tonight's large-scale event, especially because I had to see my parents, but more so because I'd always been extremely uncomfortable at formal gatherings. From the time I started going to them at a young age, I'd despised them, and as a child the only reason I hadn't complained about going was because of being able to see Bexley. But when everything happened... Well, I stopped going completely.

And no one said a damn thing because they thought I was grieving.

Despite the rumors of Bexley's death, I'd known she was still alive. In the very center of my being, I knew the truth that my friend was still out there. Now I realized that it had been the very start of our soul-fated connection. It was the only thing that had gotten me through the fact that she was missing until Gage managed to tell the two of us the truth.

Although, even that had been done in secret since the tension between clans was at an all-time high at that point. It was one of the many reasons that tonight would be so damn interesting.

"I was hoping I'd get to go longer without seeing them, but oh well," I drew out, trying to sound casual. It wasn't that I hated my parents; I respected them as exactly that—the man and woman who created me. That was it, though. There wasn't a bond or closeness between us. Our family was extremely militaristic, and my father was temperamental, always willing to jump the gun and dive into conflict.

Which was why he'd called so much. Word had no doubt reached him about a female shifted dragon at the academy, one that we were claiming as our mate. I hadn't shown any interest in women these past years, and when my parents had tried to set me up with 'suitable' shifters, I insisted that I knew who my mate was. They'd just brushed it off, though, annoyed that I was still stuck on a girl presumed dead. Or shit, maybe it was their way of trying to goad me into telling them. Jagger was right—I think our parents did suspect something.

Well, now all those suspicions would be put to rest.

"Yeah, same," Jagger murmured.

"I'm almost done!" Bexley called out to us. "I feel bad, you guys must be so bored. At least come talk to me."

Jagger chuckled at the concern in her voice, and I walked over, my gaze on Gage in the far corner of the room. He was talking quietly to someone on the phone, the prospect of tonight's events putting him on edge. There were a lot of possible ways tonight could turn out, and I knew he was speaking with security to ensure that we were fully prepared.

"Okay!" The hair stylist stepped back. "Beautiful. Now where did Amanda run off to? I swear that girl always has her head in the clouds," the woman grumbled good-naturedly, disappearing in a whirlwind to find the makeup artist. I lounged back on the sofa, Jagger going to snag a drink from the breakfast bar near Gage.

"I promise we aren't bored," I said softly. "I love watching you relax."

Bexley's gaze flashed with warmth. "I wish I was relaxed. I have a lot on my mind."

"About what Mrs. Bronzeheart told you?" I asked. We had found Bexley pretty quickly once we'd woken up, Ms. Payne pointing us in the direction of this room where an entire beauty team had been pampering our girl to the nines. It upset me to hear that she wasn't relaxed enough to fully enjoy it.

I did understand, though, especially when Bexley told us everything she'd been informed of and showed us the book Celine had made for her. Something I had no doubt she was itching to pour over.

"Not fully," Bexley answered. "I'm nervous about tonight. I'm nervous about meeting your families—or re-meeting them—and I'm worried what they'll think of me. I'm worried about everyone's reactions. I'm worried people will be mad at the Bronzehearts... I'm just worried."

Running my thumb over the dip of her brow, I caught her chin in my grasp and spoke honestly. "Everyone will be surprised but happy, I can promise you that. There may be a bit of tension about not telling everyone sooner, but no one will be upset to find out you're alive—probably the exact opposite."

Bexley sighed and nibbled her lip. "I suppose you're right."

"And as for the parents, don't think twice on that. My mom and dad both loved you when we were younger, and they don't love anyone, not even their own family. But they loved you. You were so sweet—still are—but also outspoken and opinionated, even at that age, and that's a quality my parents prize nearly as much as combat abilities."

"Well, crap. I don't have any of those," she murmured, making me chuckle. I wasn't sure that it was a completely accurate statement, though. While she didn't have formal training for fighting, I'd watched what happened with Sue, and despite the possibility of violence, Bexley had held her ground.

Courage was half the battle in combat.

"Which reminds me, how do you feel about learning some self-defense?" I watched her expression turn into amusement.

"I mean...I could try it."

"She doesn't need it," Jagger rumbled. "We can protect her."

"And we are good at that," I agreed, "but I would feel better knowing that—"

"Something like the Ioan situation can't happen again," Bexley said, her eyes flashing in determination. "You're right, I should learn some."

"Found Amanda!" the hairstylist said, rushing in before I could say anything else. "Alright boys, if you don't mind, we have about an hour until the party starts, and we need all the room we can get—Bexley's dress is sizable."

"Sizable." Bexley wiggled in her seat with excitement. "Understatement—it's like a freakin' cake or something." And I could not wait to see her in it.

I did appreciate the woman being so blunt about us leaving, even though I didn't want to. A lot of times people tiptoed around us in respect, so her directness was refreshing.

"Gage will stay in here," Jagger said, nodding towards the man in question.

He and I stood, and I dropped a kiss on Bexley's lips. "Can't wait to see your dress, *mo chuisle.*"

A pleased hum came from her throat as Jagger said something to her before following me out, the two of us instantly growing more serious as staff members rushed past, saying something about guests arriving. Instead of going towards the main entrance, we went to get ready. There was no explanation required between the two of us for why we weren't going to greet whoever's parents had shown up.

It was going to be a long enough night as it was— no need to start that shit early.

When I reached my guest suite's door, I called out to Jagger, "I'm going to head down there in about forty-five."

"I'll be ready, unfortunately."

'Unfortunately' was right...except for seeing Bexley's dress. I didn't care what it looked like, truth be told. But the way her eyes lit up in excitement? That shit was priceless.

"Breaker."

The familiar voice had me letting out a deep sigh. Jagger's gaze moved over my shoulder, his eyes narrowing just slightly in annoyance. *Yeah, I was going to bet it was my dad.* While I didn't have as much of a problem with my dad and how he raised me—with sword and shield in hand, scarring my body from a young age—Jagger and Gage had repeatedly pointed out how wrong it was. I didn't disagree with them in the least, but the past was the past.

Now I was glad for the combat skills. They would ensure that I could take care of our mate and future family by keeping them safe.

Future family. Instantly, Mrs. Bronzeheart's comments about marriage came to mind. I hadn't wanted to react to them because I wanted Bexley to have the space to decide how she felt about the situation without being influenced by us. I wanted nothing more than to marry her, but I had also been thinking about it for some time, whereas all of this was fresh and new to her. She was just learning she had three mates; I doubt she was thinking about the concept of three husbands yet.

"Father." I turned towards him, feeling so many eyes on us. Jagger and I had been standing outside of the ballroom to the side, avoiding eye contact with the guests as they arrived, many of whom were important members of our society. We were trying to avoid conversation, and doing a pretty good job of it...but now that wasn't an option. Especially with him shouting my name like that.

My father was here, and he wanted to talk—most likely to *demand* to know what was going on. I heard Jagger slip away behind me, probably to find his own parents, who'd arrived earlier. Lucky bastard. His parents may have been frustrating in their own way, but they wouldn't cause a scene like mine would.

"What the hell is this about?" he demanded. The man looked absolutely out of sorts. His light hair, like my own, was tied back, but his dark eyes were darting around rapidly, trying to get a feel for the event. One that Gage's mom had truly outdone herself for—the ballroom looked beautiful.

"You weren't picking up our calls; we got worried." My mother's voice joined his as she slipped away from staff members trying to help her. She ignored them, though, holding her own overnight bag like my dad. I think they prided themselves on being unusually difficult.

"I knew it would be easier to explain once you were here," I said, relief filling her gaze. I had no doubt she was catching on, faster than my father, that this was a celebration rather than something to be concerned about.

"The Bronzehearts told us nothing," my dad said stiffly. "Just that we needed to be here and that it was about you and your mate."

I had a feeling that Celine and Leopold enjoyed messing with my parents.

"Let's have them take your bags," I said, motioning to the staff, "so we can go into the ballroom and explain." Prioritizing an explanation over holding onto their luggage, they handed it over and then walked with me towards the massive three-story doors. I felt their surprise as we stepped into what could only be described as a spectacle of gold, bronze, silver, and black. It was tasteful and elegant, yet more grand than I had imagined was possible. Lively music was already playing, and the ballroom was packed with eager guests waiting for information on what was happening.

They wouldn't have to wait for long.

"Darla!" Gage's mom appeared out of nowhere and gave my mom a hug, one she immediately returned. While my father didn't realize it, I had a feeling the moms had been talking even during the intense tension between clans. Considering they'd been close through most of our childhood, I could hardly blame them.

"This is beautiful," my mom gushed uncharacteristically before seeming to catch herself. "But what is this about? If it's my son's mate, why are you hosting—"

"Two minutes," Celine said, offering an understanding look to my dad, clearly sensing his impatience. "Two minutes and everything will be answered. Please take a seat and relax at the front table; the Silvershades are already there with Leopold. Breaker, the other two are up front by the side door if you'd like to join them."

The side door that Bexley would be walking through.

"On it." I offered both my parents a look. "Like she said, two minutes." I had no doubt they would be complaining for the entirety of those one hundred and twenty seconds.

As I walked towards Gage and Jagger, my gaze strayed towards the pair of french doors that were currently closed. I could feel that Bexley was near, though, and I was so damn eager to see her. I hated being apart, even if it had been less than two hours.

"How are they?" I asked Jagger, referring to his parents.

"Reserved and waiting to see what's happening," he said dryly. "They are reacting exactly as you would expect."

"I think that my parents were right to do this as soon as possible," Gage murmured. "Rumors spread so damn fast—this could have led to a much larger conflict if we'd waited."

I couldn't have agreed more.

When the ballroom doors closed and the music softened, my gaze moved towards Celine and Leopold standing at the front of the room.

"Thank you all for coming!" Celine said with a welcoming smile. "I know many of you are confused about why we've asked you here tonight."

Murmured agreements reached our ears as I heard the side door open, and my chest constricted as a rumble left my throat.

Bexley.

My perfect fucking Bexley.

She was a vision in an obsidian ball gown that was tucked at the waist and then went out in a skirt that turned gold where it brushed the floor. She looked ethereal, like something out of a fantasy, and when her eyes met mine, a blush rushed to her cheeks, making me know my expression was revealing exactly how I felt.

And I knew the moment when guests began to notice her because an awed silence fell on the crowd.

"Tonight," Celine continued, "we celebrate three very important young men in our territory finding their mate—the lost heir of the Flash Clan, Bexley Blackforge."

Chapter Fifteen

Bexley Blackforge

I had thought, especially after talking to Breaker, that I was somewhat prepared for what I would face walking into this event...but I was wrong. I was so wrong, and now I stood frozen, halfway towards my mates, looking over the giant ballroom in awe and a bit of fear.

So many eyes were on me.

In any normal circumstance, I would have been thrilled to be here. The room was beautiful, decorated in metallic tones that directly reminded me of my mates. The soft music in the background was renditions of some of my favorite classical pieces, and the familiar faces of the Bronzehearts and my mates made my chest squeeze with happiness.

It was everything else that made me feel fear.

The shock of everyone in the crowd, some faces

familiar but most not, had my stomach feeling queasy. It felt like everyone was studying me, analyzing me, in response to the Bronzehearts' words, and my biggest fear was that they found me...*lacking*. The breath whooshed out of me as I considered turning and walking out.

"Bexley."

Gage's voice had my heart slowing. Before he'd spoken, the furious beat had been distracting me from the fact that my mates had been trying to get my attention. Meeting his gaze and then looking towards Breaker and Jagger, I felt significantly better at the softness, affection, and understanding there. I knew I could trust them, and if they thought I would be okay in this situation, that I would be safe, then I would believe it.

Celine continued speaking to the crowd, but I couldn't hear her—not until I was wrapped in the embrace of my three mates. I walked toward them, trying not to rush, and Breaker immediately wrapped a large arm around my center, standing behind me, as Jagger intertwined the fingers of my right hand with his. Gage stood slightly in front of me and off to the side just enough that it wasn't super obvious what he was doing.

I knew, though. I knew he was shielding me from the eyes of everyone in the room. Although, I wasn't positive that he needed to do that. Most of the people here were staring at me in surprise and awe, without an ounce of ridicule or anger. It went a long way to making me feel more secure about their acceptance.

And I found that I did want them to accept me. If this was a gathering of community members that were important to my mates, then I wanted them to like me as well.

"I don't understand," a man from the front circular table finally spoke up, drawing my attention. "I don't understand *how* this is possible—the Blackforge family, including their daughter, were killed. We all saw the aftermath. Every single one of us laid witness to the betrayal that took place."

The woman next to him nodded fiercely, and a wave of grief ran over me, taking me off guard. Of course the idea of what happened to my family had always saddened me, but this felt different. This felt like the memory of an emotion I'd felt before, now uncovered and overwhelming everything for a split second.

I blinked, trying to not overthink it, as I noticed the woman's gaze had moved to me. There was a softness to her eyes that I wouldn't have expected, although based on what Breaker had told me earlier, maybe I should have.

It didn't take me long at all to realize that they

were Breaker's parents. The man looked very similar to him, his light hair tied back and his formalwear looking far more like a suit of armor than anything else. The woman had gold eyes, and her brown hair was pulled up in an elegant twist, but her dress was simple—very different from most of the other women here and for sure different from myself. I didn't think she minded, though. In fact, by the way they held themselves alone, I got the distinct impression that both of them took pride in their simplicity and the serious nature of their personalities.

"A private discussion between the three families is needed following tonight," Leopold agreed, looking at another couple that bore a striking resemblance to Jagger. Their expressions were reserved, staring at the Bronzehearts with a clinical and searching gaze.

"But right now we are going to celebrate the fact that our three sons have been reunited with their fated mate," Celine said with a steely expression, as if daring anyone to disagree with her. "Something that we all suspected when they were younger. So let's welcome Bexley back into our community and take a moment to appreciate being all together once again after eight years."

Right on cue, the music picked up again and everyone in the crowd applauded, some standing and others talking animatedly with those at their table. They didn't seem nearly as caught up or worried about the situation; in fact, they just seemed excited. They were taking Celine's words at face value, and the only people who seemed truly confused and worried were the other two clan families. Not that I blamed them.

A girl who was supposed to be dead shows up in the public eye after having been 'missing' for eight years and is now the joint mate to three of the most powerful shifters in Trabea? They had a right to be worried and suspicious, even if it made me a bit sad.

"Come on." Breaker squeezed my waist. "Better to get the reintroduction done now before my parents lose their minds."

Jagger hummed softly in agreement. "I have to admit, Gage, your parents are really good at managing both of our families."

Gage didn't respond though, looking stressed while examining my face. I had a feeling that the only thing upsetting Gage was the prospect of me being upset—I don't think he gave a flying fate whether or not the parents were upset.

"I'm good," I promised him, not wanting him to be distressed over my state. "Just trying to sort through how I feel about all of this."

He nodded in understanding, and as we walked

over towards the parents, Breaker's father was the first to turn at our approach.

"No warning. No warning at all," his father bit out towards his son, making me tense.

"Stop. Now," Breaker warned in a sudden flare of dominance. "Do not use that tone around her."

His father's eyes darkened in surprise before his gaze moved to me, analyzing my face and looking for *something*. I stood there, frozen, not knowing exactly how to react.

Unlike the other shifters at our school, it was clear he was a dragon and a very strong one, so my normal confidence was lacking a bit. I also cared about my mates, and I didn't want to risk their parents not liking me since we were going to be in each other's lives for...well, hopefully forever. That concept once again had me feeling that giddy sense of nervousness that had hit me when Celine brought up marriage.

"It *is* her," Breaker's father grunted and looked at his wife, who was offering me a soft smile.

"Of course it is, Trek," the woman said, her hardened features softening. "Bexley is perfectly unique. Always has been. There is no mistaking her."

"It's nice to meet both of you." I kept my voice soft, both of them staring at me in surprise and confusion. I didn't understand why until Breaker spoke up.

"She has no memories from before being found by the Bronzehearts," he explained. "In fact, until she shifted this weekend, she couldn't think of anything about her previous life without extreme pain, so she doesn't remember any of you."

The shock on their faces was echoed by another voice that held a surprising amount of emotion. "I don't understand how that's possible, how any of this happened. We thought...we thought we'd lost her." It was Jagger's mom who was talking, her face contorted in concern as the Bronzehearts joined the conversation.

"My husband and son found her in an alleyway in the city near our border," Celine said. "We thought it best to bring her back with us because we still had no idea what had happened and who was to blame. When we realized that she not only had no memories but that she would black out in pain if any topic related to her past or her being a dragon was brought up, we decided to keep her existence quiet until we could figure out how to fix it. We didn't want to cause her any unnecessary pain."

She wasn't wrong—the time or two that the other families had been brought up over the years had sent me reeling, so seeing them in person would have most likely been excruciating.

"So it wasn't because you didn't trust us," Jagger's father said dryly, his silver hair and dark eyes a direct contrast to his wife. The two were a perfect pair, and the combination was literally Jagger. They were a stunning family.

"I think we were all confused on who to trust," Leopold reminded them, "but I suggest we save this conversation for later since we still don't know who attacked the Blackforges that night. There could be a traitor in one of our clans, and until we know…"

Everyone seemed to agree on that measure, and I took the moment to explain from my perspective. "I'm slowly gaining memories back, so I apologize for not remembering any of you. I know this is probably confusing—"

"Do not apologize," Jagger said gently, placing a reassuring hand on the small of my back.

"He's right," Jagger's mom said. "You have no need to apologize. I'm sorry our reactions are causing you distress. My name is Marilyn, and this is my husband Arnold. It's wonderful to see you again, Bexley."

"You as well," I whispered, unable to help the emotion that swept through me.

Something tugged on the back of my mind,

telling me that these people were important to me, and despite feeling like I was meeting them anew, there was also a sense of comfort around them that reminded me a lot of how I felt around the Bronze-hearts when I'd first arrived at their estate.

It also told me one important thing—they hadn't been the ones to attack my family. I just knew it. I didn't know *how* I knew, but I knew without a doubt that it wasn't one of the other clans. But then who was it? My chest squeezed with the reminder that there was a very possible threat to my mates and my life, which was only now right on the cusp of truly starting.

"If all of you don't mind," Gage spoke up, clearly realizing I was caught up in my thoughts, "I would like to get Bexley some fresh air. We'll be back shortly for dinner."

Without waiting for a response, my mates led me away from the cluster of parents. I exhaled in relief, only now realizing the extent of the tension that had been running through me since entering the room. We stepped through a set of side doors, the cold autumn breeze running over my skin, before turning a corner and moving us out of sight. I buried my face against Gage's chest as the warmth from my mates' large frames kept me comfortable and insulated.

"You did amazing," he murmured.

I pulled back and spoke honestly. "It's...it's just a lot, and I hate seeing the surprise and hurt on people's faces when they realize I don't remember them. I feel horrible."

"The minute you want to leave, we can," Jagger said quietly. I loved that he was willing to walk away from all of this. I knew it wasn't the solution, though.

"But I don't think anyone minds once they're told about the situation," Breaker assured me. "In fact, my parents have handled all of this surprisingly well. They don't like surprises," he added. *I'd caught on to that pretty quickly.*

"Okay." I exhaled and then nodded. "I'm ready to go back inside..." My stomach suddenly rumbled, making me flush. "Plus, I'm hungry. Those little sandwiches I ate while getting ready didn't do much."

"I should have brought you more," Breaker grumbled.

"They thought it would get on my dress or mess up my makeup," I explained.

"Fucking ridiculous." Jagger frowned. "Makeup can be redone, and a dress can be fixed—"

"But a hungry Bexley cannot."

I snorted at Gage's words, and as we walked in, the servers for dinner began to make their rounds. I was so eager to eat that I didn't overthink the fact that all the parents would be sitting at the same table with us for dinner.

When we got to the table, there was much less tension than before, and when I looked over at Celine, she offered me a knowing wink. I had no idea what she had said or done, but *clearly* something had been fixed.

Chapter Sixteen

Bexley Blackforge

"I can't dance anymore, my feet will fall off!" I insisted. Breaker chuckled, easily lifting me. We waltzed across the floor, his easy and practiced movements making me know that he had his fair share of dance lessons, much like Gage and myself.

I normally loved dancing, at least with Gage who always managed to catch me before I tripped over my own two feet, but I wasn't lying when I said I was absolutely *danced out*.

In what I was pretty sure was an effort to prevent me being approached by party guests, my mates had kept me busy on the dance floor, the other two always fielding anyone trying to be too invasive with their questioning.

Which there had been a fair amount of. I don't

think it had been with evil or malicious intent, I think people were sort of busybodies. And to be fair, this entire event was centered around the public announcement that I was...well, *alive*.

Questions weren't that surprising.

"I can't let you off this dance floor unless you're ready to leave the party," Breaker rumbled. "I'm too worried I'll end up snapping someone's wrist."

"The hair touching was unsettling," I agreed. At least three people had tried to touch my hair tonight. I mean, I may have been sheltered, but even I knew that was inappropriate behavior, especially with someone you've only just met.

"Honestly, I'm pretty tired," I said, answering his question. "I wouldn't mind going back to the room."

"I can assist with that." Jagger appeared out of thin air, telling Breaker, "You should go with Gage. The dads are going to have a talk, and the moms disappeared about twenty minutes ago. I've got Bexley."

"Maybe I wanted to be part of the"—I stifled a yawn—"talks."

Before, I would have been worried he saw me as a burden to watch, but I knew differently now. I knew that was the farthest thought from Jagger's mind.

"Boring shit," Breaker assured before kissing me

lightly. "We're sleeping in your room tonight, even if we have to sneak out in the morning."

"Sounds perfect to me," I sang out as Jagger pulled me into his arms. I let out a happy hum at the embrace he wrapped me in.

"How are you feeling?" he asked softly, tilting my jaw up.

"Like I want to go back to the room, take a long bath, and cuddle," I answered honestly, letting out a small giggle as he swept me up into his arms. Luckily, we didn't run into anyone wanting to talk on the way out, everyone seeming to have gotten the message that we were leaving. I buried my head against his neck as he held me in a bridal hold, his grip secure and comforting.

I would love to say that I didn't almost doze off while in his arms, but that would be a lie. The emotional turmoil of the past few hours, paired with the excitement and nervousness, would be enough to exhaust anyone.

When we reached my suite, Jagger sat me down on the couch and disappeared into the bedroom. I heard him turn on the bathwater, and I lazily reached down to undo my shoes, the gold heels sparkling beneath the warm lighting of the sconces lining the walls.

When I finally managed to get my heels off,

Jagger was walking around the room and closing the curtains to all the french doors, and even the ones for the door that connected me to the rest of the estate. It wasn't something I normally did, but considering the amount of strangers on the estate tonight I appreciated the gesture, including his final precaution of flicking the lock.

"Up you go," Jagger said, lifting me by the waist and setting me on the ground. I winced at the feel of my feet hitting the floor, and when I tried to walk, I grumbled, my skirt catching underneath me.

"This thing is a safety hazard," he muttered, walking behind me as his fingers trailed the zipper. "You looked beautiful in it though."

"Celine always knows exactly what I want to wear. I swear, it's a magic power," I said as he unzipped the dress. The weight of it fell off me, and I stepped out of the masterpiece of a garment and wrapped my arms around myself, a light blush touching my cheeks. I knew I was still wearing a black strapless bra and a slip skirt, but the way Jagger's gaze ran over me made me feel like I was wearing far less.

"Bath." His rough voice had my toes curling as he ushered me towards the bathroom. I smiled up at him, seeing that he'd added my favorite pink bubble bath to the water.

"You weren't lying about the sparkles," he mused, looking around at the decor.

"Isn't it fun to look at?" I sighed happily. "I know it's not realistic to have everything be this sparkly, but a bathroom and maybe a kitchen wouldn't be the worst thing in the world."

"I think that's doable," he said, his lips pressing up in amusement. "Alright, in you go. I'm going to get you some food."

"Cupcakes," I said, giving him a large-eyed, pleading look. "Cupcakes, please."

"Some real food also," he countered.

I nibbled my lip in thought. "Cupcakes...and a grilled cheese. My final offer."

He barked out a laugh I rarely heard before dropping a kiss on my nose. "Alright, little treasure. I accept."

With that he was out of the room, and I couldn't help but feel a bit of pride for making him laugh. Slipping out of the rest of my clothes, I sank into my bubble bath and let out a content hum, the sudsy warm water running over my skin, especially my feet, in a soothing and relaxing way.

It took only minutes for the tension to completely leave my body as I leaned back in the tub, allowing the water to cover everything up to my chin. My hair, which was piled on top of my head, and my face were the only parts of me out of the water, and it was absolutely divine. That was exactly how Jagger found me.

"You look like you're nearly asleep," he mused, coming to sit down on the marble floor by the tub.. "Food is on its way, so try to hold out a bit."

"Is Ms. Payne working tonight?" I frowned. "She should be taking tonight off. She and Mr. Webb don't relax nearly as much as they should. They're always together, doing one thing or another."

"Oh, I think they relax plenty," Jagger countered, "considering they live together."

I stared at him in shock. "What? They freakin' live together?!"

"Yeah." He chuckled softly. "Gage said they've been together for a few years now. They live in the staff housing on the estate, but apparently in the same house."

"Oh my fates," I murmured as I tried to think back on all their interactions. "That makes so much sense."

"I'm surprised they haven't told you." Jagger arched his brow.

"I'm surprised I didn't put it together," I countered. "Well, not that surprised," I amended with a sigh. "I mean, I didn't even realize Gage liked me until days ago."

"And I don't feel like he was very good at hiding it," Jagger added.

"I think," I drew out in thought, smiling, "that he blamed most of it on his dragon...which I guess could partially be true."

"And mostly an excuse," Jagger said. "Though our dragons do make us do some crazy shit sometimes. I'm waiting until yours starts up."

"Starts up with what?" I asked curiously.

"Doing things like scenting us, or getting possessive over other—"

"Oh, that's happened," I whispered. "I just was trying to not react."

"Feel free to react, little treasure." His eyes flashed with heat. "I love the idea of you being possessive—although you never have a reason to worry."

"I just don't like other women looking at you," I murmured, dipping my gaze down to the bubbles.. "I was worried you'd think I was weird for getting upset about that."

"Most natural thing in the world," he assured me, running a thumb over my lip.

When a knock sounded on the main door to my suite, Jagger's eyes lit up. "That'll be your food," he said, pressing a soft kiss to my lips before disappearing. My stomach rumbled at the thought of eating, so

I quickly washed up and rinsed off my makeup, reluctantly stepping out of the hot water and wrapping myself up in a robe, purely in the pursuit of cupcakes.

And man did I find some.

Gold and silver pearlized cupcakes sat on a plate near two grilled cheese sandwiches and some water. The fire in my bedroom was crackling, and Jagger had the television on some news station. I probably should've paid more attention to what was going on in our territory, but I found myself distracted far too often to listen to them.

In this case, my distraction came in the form of food.

Curled up on the bed, I finished eating both sandwiches before adding two cupcakes to the mix. With my eyes heavy enough they were closing, it was absolutely no surprise when I fell asleep. What was surprising, though, was the dream I was met with.

"Jagger?" My voice was shaky as I looked around the garden, trying to find him. I knew he'd walked out here upset about something, and it felt like it was my fault. I wasn't sure what I'd done though. Or maybe he wasn't upset at me... His glare had been at Ben, but that didn't make sense either.

"Go back inside. Please." Jagger's voice was rough, and as I turned the corner, I found him on a bench, his head bent and elbows on his knees.

In the past year, since his birthday, he'd gotten a lot taller. So much so that it felt like he was at least a full head taller than me, if not two. It was a lot harder to look him in the eye now.

"What's wrong?" I asked softly, a nervous energy surrounding me. My stomach churned uncomfortably as his icy gaze met mine.

"What's wrong? What's wrong, Bex, is that Ben doesn't know when to go the fuck away."

"His family is here to visit," I pointed out, slightly surprised by his swearing. "He probably just wants to make friends."

I didn't know Ben well, but his family and mine were working out some trading deal that would allow his pack to do business within our lands, so they were here for the weekend. Ben seemed lonely, so I'd felt like we needed to include him, but now I was wondering if that was a mistake.

"He doesn't want to be friends with you," Jagger growled softly, running a hand through his hair in frustration. "Friendship is the last thing he wants."

Walking forward, I sat down on the bench next to him and smoothed a hand over his back. The tension seemed to instantly release from his frame as he *sagged in what appeared to be defeat. "If you don't like him, then we don't have to hang out with him. I want to hang out with you, Jagger, not him."*

Plus, despite feeling bad for him, Ben sort of freaked me out. He kept touching my hair, but not in the nice way one of my friends did, where they would sometimes braid it for me when we were outside, or when we were watching a movie and they would brush it for me. No...this was different, and didn't make me feel good at all.

Jagger nodded and squeezed my hand, staring down at it in thought before responding. "I just don't like the way he looks at you."

"Well, then I don't want anything to do with him." I rested my head against his shoulder. "I may feel bad that he's bored, but I'm not looking for new friends. I already have three amazing ones."

The kiss he pressed to the top of my head made my chest flutter in a way I didn't understand but absolutely loved.

"Bexley."

My eyes flew open, and I found myself pinned beneath Jagger's hard body, his shirtless chest pressed to my own. My eyes widened in realization that my robe had slipped open and I was, for all intents and purposes, naked...and underneath my mate. My mate, who looked like he was in pain, his forehead against mine and his brow contorted as if focusing.

For just a moment, though, none of that mattered. Instead, all I could focus on was the surge of intense emotions rolling through me. My eyes pricked with tears as the dream I had seemed to unlock a series of memories, flashes in time, every single one of them featuring Jagger.

"Fuck, I'm sorry—"

I seared my lips against his, interrupting him and wanting him to understand that I wasn't upset—far from it, despite not being able to verbally communicate that—but when I pulled back with tears on my face, I could see the panic in his eyes.

"Not upset," I reassured him in an awed whisper when I could finally talk. "I had a dream about us. You were upset about Ben or something, but now I'm remembering all sorts of stuff about us. It's amazing and a bit overwhelming. I'm not upset, I promise."

Surprise and then relief coated his face. He pulled me up, tucking my robe around me as he cupped my jaw, his study of my face filled with cautious hope. "What do you remember?"

Closing my eyes, I tried to recall the flashes of moments. Running through the garden, laughing during tutoring, holding hands during events when I could feel he was on edge, watching movies together. While they were small snippets, I relayed every detail that I could, his body filled with tension as he hung onto my every word. More than anything, though, past any details or memories, there was a fusion of emotions that came from how I felt about Jagger now and the love I had for him then.

Because I *had* loved him then. There was no question about it.

My eyes opened, wet with tears as I spoke softly. "I can't believe I forgot so much, and I can tell there's so much more. I can't imagine what it was like knowing that I'd forgotten you. I am so sorry, Jagger."

"Hey," he whispered, his expression intense. "Don't you dare say sorry. You lost your memory through no fault of your own, in an effort by your parents to protect you. I would take that one hundred times over you being put in danger. Besides, we found each other again. I will always find you, Bexley. I promise."

I believed him. I think I'd known when I bumped into him during the exam day that there had been something special between us. Something I hadn't yet understood.

Deciding to not hold myself back, I surged forward and melded my lips to his in a desperate, needy kiss. My fingers strung through his hair, and I was flat on my back once again, my robe falling open.

Jagger let out a groan, pulling back from the kiss. "*This* was why I was waking you up. I have zero control when it comes to you," he rumbled. "I woke up to you half-naked and on top of me. It was pure fucking torture, and I didn't trust myself."

"Doesn't sound like a bad thing to me," I said breathlessly. I loved the feeling of him positioned over me like this, keeping me pinned to the bed.

"Bad only for you," he growled, the low vibration of his voice making my toes curl. "You have no idea what I want to do to you, little treasure."

I had a feeling it wasn't bad at all, but now I was *very* interested in knowing.

"Show me," I whispered, my voice a near plea. My words caused the intensity in his eyes to grow, making it so they were nearly glowing. I whimpered, trying to press my legs together, but his large frame stopped me. The cool air from the room on my body didn't help, either—everything felt heightened, and it was driving me absolutely crazy.

"Hands up," he ordered, nipping my lip. "Grip the pillow above you and don't move. If you move, I stop."

I didn't know what he planned to do, but I knew I wouldn't want him to stop. Jagger had the ability to give me euphoric pleasure, and that was the connection I needed to him right now. The more memories that flooded in, showing the history I had with this amazing man, the more I wanted to be closer to him.

He ran his lips down my skin, soft kisses and teasing nibbles. My core tightened and my breath caught at the feel of his lips against my flesh. His hands gripped my waist, keeping me pinned as he moved down my body, his lips tracing the swell of my breast—

"Jagger," I moaned as his mouth teased my nipple. I could feel my wet heat coating my thighs, and my head felt dizzy with the need coursing through me.

"Don't move those hands," he growled softly against my skin. "I don't have enough control to have you touch me while my lips are on you—not unless you want to get fucked."

I really didn't mind the sound of that.

My hips bucked up as he continued to kiss down my stomach, and my legs fell open of their own accord as he grew close to my center. My breath caught momentarily, realizing just how wet I was and wondering if I should be embarrassed.

"Fates," Jagger groaned. "Fuck, you smell so fucking perfect. Look at how wet you are."

My gaze tracked his fingers as he sat back,

running his thick digits over my slit and causing me to gasp. When he pulled his soaked fingers up and popped them in his mouth, a whimper slipped from my lips.

His eyes closed as he groaned, a deep rattling sound coming from his chest that had me nearly trembling, needing his touch and his lips back on me. When his eyes opened, his gaze was nearly feral, and a whisper of his name left my lips.

Then his mouth was on me. A cry of pleasure left me as he absolutely devoured me, his mouth teasing and toying with my center, his tongue running from my clit down to my slit. The noises coming out of him were animalistic, and his grip on my hips was tight and unyielding. My eyes were closed, my fingers digging into the pillow so hard that I worried I would rip it apart. I didn't want him to stop, though. I would die if he did.

Suddenly worried at the prospect, my hands left the pillow and tightened in his hair, holding him to me. He groaned, pulling back and offering me a wild look. I nearly whimpered as I realized I'd broken his rule.

"I should stop," he gritted out. "But you taste way too fucking good."

"Jagger!" I cried out as he went back to his teasing pace, his tongue pressing into my center. An electric pulse hit my clit, causing my thighs to tremble.

"You can make it up to me by coming on my tongue, little treasure."

His rough words had my eyes rolling back into my head as everything *exploded*. I cried out his name, my hands gripping his hair as a rumbling sound left his chest, filling the room with a spark of magic that made me feel like I was floating.

Pleasure pulsed through each limb of my body, and when I felt like I was finally coming down, my hands released from his hair.

Jagger sat back, and in my dazed state, I watched as he released his erection, keeping one hand on my thigh to hold my legs open and the other on his hard length. He stroked it, and I watched, mesmerized, as he ran his gaze over my body before grunting out his own release.

His hot cum landed between my legs, coating my wet center and mixing our releases. The marking was so primal, and it had something in the center of my chest lighting up, demanding that we do the same, but more.

Running on pure instinct, I sat up, Jagger surging forward and meeting my lips in a hard kiss before laying me flat on the bed. He rolled us so that I was on top, his shaft pressed right between my legs as I teased his lips with mine. I rolled my hips against him, loving the pained groan that left his lips as I worked my way down his jaw and to his throat, his grip tightening to bruising on my waist as if he was afraid I'd try to leave.

Then I did something I would have never expected—I bit Jagger.

My teeth pulsed and my magic exploded out from my chest as I bit his neck hard, breaking the skin. An inhuman sound left him as his magic broke free and joined mine, filling the room with a dangerous and electric energy. Thunder cracked in the distance, and the sound sent an exhilarating sensation across my skin. The obsidian threads of my magic that had been dancing between Jagger's silver ones tightened into a hard, rope-like bond. Something snapped inside of me, and the release of that tension, the unspoken worry about not being bonded to my mate, faded.

I had marked Jagger as my mate. Holy fates.

Chapter Seventeen

Bexley Blackforge

W hen I woke up, it was late morning and my entire body was melted against the mattress. My feet and muscles were sore from the night before, but there was a smile on my face because all of that was over-shadowed by the remnants of pleasure still coursing through me, not only because of Jagger's mouth but because of the mark I'd left on him. The one that I'd instinctively placed in the heat of the moment.

Once the fog of lust had cleared from my mind, I'd immediately felt bad for biting him, concerned that Jagger would be upset that I hadn't asked him first. *How wrong I'd been.*

. . .

"Jagger, I'm sorry, I should have—" I whispered, feeling slightly panicked in realization of what I'd done. I should've asked. I absolutely should have asked him if that was okay—

"Bexley." I was rolled flat on my back, my hands pinned above me. Jagger's gaze was wild and filled with so much heat that it made me feel like my body was being dipped in molten lava. The one thing I didn't see was anger.

"Do not second-guess yourself, and do not apologize. Just tell me that you meant it. Tell me that you wanted to mark me as your mate."

My entire body relaxed at his request, my gaze holding his as I nodded, a smile flitting to my lips. My gaze moved to the bite mark on his neck, the sight flooding me with an indescribable feeling of love, security, happiness, comfort, desire, and probably a thousand other things I couldn't name. "Of course I wanted to mark you, I just felt bad for not asking."

Pride and satisfaction filled his gaze as he brushed his nose against mine. "You never have to ask if you want to mark or touch me. There will never be a time that I don't want your claim or your touch."

His words had filled me with confidence, instantly removing any lingering doubts about what I'd done and allowing me to enjoy the primal satisfaction at the idea of marking him. *I just wished he'd marked me as well.*

Sitting up in bed, I let out a big yawn, stretching my arms above my head while looking around. Where the heck were my mates? Frowning, I slid out of bed, feeling a bit odd to be waking up in my old room again. I loved it, but I missed the dorms. More so, I missed waking up with my mates. Maybe we would be able to go back today now that we were done with the event? Especially if DIA was increasing security.

A feminine voice reached me as the door suddenly opened a crack, Jagger slipping in from the main room of my suite. He crooked a finger at me, and I nearly flew across the room into his arms and buried my head against his chest, his lips brushing the top of my head.

"My mom and Celine are in the other room talking—prepare yourself." He said it like a warning, but I got the feeling he wasn't all that concerned. In fact, he seemed amused. "The others are getting ready for us to leave."

"We're going back?" I smiled, unable to rein in my excitement.

He nodded. "We got word that security has been increased, and classes will start back tomorrow, so if there's a time to go back, it's now. Plus," Jagger rumbled, "I want us back in our dorm."

And I loved the sound of that.

"They should absolutely not go back," said Mrs. Silvershade in a calm, controlled tone as we stepped into the main room of my suite. Her gaze darted to me and her son in concern, and I could tell she was way more worried than she was expressing. "Bexley, good morning."

"Morning," I said softly. "What's wrong?"

Mrs. Silvershade looked back at Celine, both of them dressed for the day. I was starting to wonder if I should have at least brushed my teeth...

"It's one thing for a sector to deal with some security issues, but multiple? Within the first week of school? Come on, Celine."

"Bex," Celine said, pointing towards a tray of iced coffee, "please help yourself. And Marilyn, I completely hear you, but our sons are grown and we can't tell them what to do."

"Mom," Jagger said, his voice soft. There was that note to it that indicated she wasn't acting the way he expected. Was she normally not like this? "If they have an increase in security, I'm sure it's fine."

"*Fine* isn't *safe*," she countered, her brow dipping as she turned back to Celine. "You know as well as I do that this is big. It's one thing for the boys to go back, but Bexley just returned to us."

"We are perfectly capable of keeping her safe," Gage said as he walked in, followed by Breaker and his mom.

"It isn't about that," Celine drew out in defense of Marilyn. "The bigger issue is that I don't want to deprive Bexley of the experience of going to the academy. I know how much this means to her."

Finally reaching the cart with iced coffee, I grabbed some and turned to find all of them staring at me as if waiting for an answer.

"I *do* want to go back," I said. "I even have new classes, some of which are with the guys. I don't want to hide away."

I wasn't positive where that last thought had come from, but it resonated as true inside of me. I felt an odd sense of duty to defend those who couldn't defend themselves, even if it meant a challenge.

"More so," I continued, feeling the need to explain myself, "there are shifters that need someone to defend them from threats *inside* the school."

"Defend them? Who?" Breaker's mom asked, her confused expression mirrored by Mrs. Silvershade. Celine was drinking her iced coffee, seemingly unsurprised by what I was saying.

"Prey shifters," I explained. "I don't like how it's

a free-for-all to bully them. I already had to stop one girl this week. It's ridiculous."

"Bexley stepped in to save two prey shifters from a snake shifter that was trying to hurt them," Breaker said. Both moms looked at me in surprise.

"I want to be there to make sure nothing else happens. I can't just leave if no one else is going to defend them." The surety in my voice was far more prominent than I expected, and I saw a flash of pride in Mrs. Firespell's gaze.

"Well, that settles it. There's no talking her out of it; I can tell."

Celine put down her iced coffee on the table. "I agree since as a dragon, specifically a storm dragon, Bexley can do that. She has that power."

"I don't fully understand it," Jagger's mom said, joining the conversation, "nor do I think it's your responsibility. You have far larger things to focus on, but I also don't disagree that unnecessary violence should be stopped. If you think that's the right move, then we have to trust you."

The support from all three of them had me feeling like I was doing something right, even if I had already felt confident in it.

"If the security threats grow, we'll come back," Jagger assured her.

"We would never put Bexley in unnecessary danger," Breaker agreed.

"Okay," Mrs. Silvershade whispered. "Just be careful."

"We will," I promised.

"Now." Celine stood, looking satisfied. "Let's leave them to get ready. I wanted to talk to you two about something before they leave anyway."

Mrs. Silvershade's gaze lit up as if she knew what Celine wanted to discuss, and Mrs. Firespell nodded, not surprised in the least. As they walked out, the door closing behind them, I offered my mates a curious look. "What are they going to talk about?"

"Probably wedding shit," Gage murmured, making my ears heat.

"Everyone keeps bringing up weddings." I drew in my lip, my gaze darting to all three of them. "Is that...is that something you guys want? I mean, obviously in the future, not right now."

Gage's brows dipped in confusion, and Breaker chuckled. "That's not even in question. We absolutely want that."

Oh.

Jagger walked up to me and kissed the top of my head. "You marked me as your mate—that's bigger than any wedding."

"She marked you?" Breaker was immediately up and rounding me, pinning me between the two of them. His eyes were filled with a bit of envy but mostly curiosity. Although Jagger's smug smirk didn't help.

"Yeah, she did."

I couldn't help but smile at how happy he was. For a minute I was so caught up in their reactions and the possessive way Breaker had looped an arm around me that I hadn't realized Gage was still staring at me in confusion.

"What?" I asked softly.

"Just trying to figure out where I went wrong that you had to ask that question." He ran a hand through his hair.

"The marriage one?" My brows went up. "Of course I'm going to freaking ask."

Gage approached so that I was completely surrounded by my mates, his finger running over my lip. "Of course I want to marry you. You've been using my last name for years."

I had been. My cheeks flared with heat, thinking about how much I'd loved seeing the name *Bexley Bronzeheart* on my entrance letter.

"Something that will change," Jagger muttered. Apparently he didn't want 'Bronzeheart' to be the only last name I had... At least, I think that was where he was going with it.

"You literally have her mark on your neck," Gage rumbled. "You have no reason to be jealous, ever."

Was that really how he viewed it? Was my mark that valuable to him? Feeling hot in the face, the overwhelming wave of emotions at the sincerity in his voice hit me as I slipped from between them and put my hands on my face, staring at them in surprise.

"Okay, I need more coffee before we talk about any of this," I grumbled, walking over to grab my glass of iced coffee from where I'd set it down. Taking a big sip, I turned to find all of them staring at me in amusement. "Seriously! No wedding talk before two cups of coffee."

That'd give me a moment to temper my reactions so I didn't act like a total dork about it. Seriously, I was two seconds away from bursting into a confetti shower of excitement because of how much they liked me. Though I guessed in this situation, saying they *liked* me seemed like a bit of an understatement.

Then again, the word *like* seemed a bit more reasonable than...well, I wasn't going to think about that word yet. I was jumping the gun. Right? That's what normal people would say... But why didn't it feel that way with them?

Breaker sighed. "We should probably get packed up anyway."

"When are we leaving?" I asked.

"As soon as possible," Gage said.

"I do want to make a stop at one of the stores on our way out though," Jagger admitted. "The downtown district hasn't changed around here, right?"

"No." Gage arched his brow, as if trying to figure out why he would need to stop there.

"I'll go get ready!" I announced, walking towards the bathroom and leaving them to talk about whatever plan they had.

Humming happily, I took a quick shower, wrapping myself in a robe as I stepped out. Turning on my curling iron, I brushed my teeth and applied light makeup, telling myself I didn't need to do *all* the steps today. We had no classes, so I was hoping we could have a cozy day inside.

After placing a few loose curls in my hair, I walked out of my bedroom, finding it empty. I got dressed quickly, throwing on a pair of light wash jeans with boots and an off-the-shoulder sweater before packing up my bag. I hadn't taken out much—Celine ensured I had everything I'd needed to get ready for the event—so it was fairly easy. When everything was packed, I pulled the weekend bag over my shoulder and walked into the main room.

"Ready to go, cupcake?" Gage asked, his eyes warm as he looked over me, heat infusing his green gaze with bronze. I wasn't positive when he'd gotten in here, but he was leaning against the island with a box of cupcakes in his hands.

"Are those Ms. Payne's cupcakes?" I asked, my voice pitched with excitement.

"Yes." He chuckled, trading them for my bag. I held the precious cargo securely as the two of us made our way to the main part of the house.

Intertwining my hand with his free one, I asked, "Last night went well, right? I'm trying to not over-think it, but I wasn't sure how I was supposed to act, to be honest."

He squeezed my hand. "You did amazing. There wasn't a way to mess it up, Bexley—people were just thrilled to see that you were okay after all this time."

I knew he was right, and honestly, except for a few weird moments, everyone had been extremely welcoming. Although there was one person I was worried about, and as we approached the main entrance, I realized that he and all the other parents were waiting to see us off.

"You have no reason to be worried about any of them," Gage assured me. "Anything they may be worked up over is their own damn problem."

Breaker's father was the first to look away from the conversation he was having with his son. I must have had my emotions painted across my face because his wince in reaction was noticeable.

Everyone else was talking, but as if he knew the problem, Gage led me right up to Breaker and his father.

I knew the man probably didn't mean anything by it, but he seemed not only the most intimidating, but the most aggressively upset about Breaker not telling him about me sooner.

"Bexley—"

"You can call me Bex," I insisted softly.

"Bex, then." Breaker's father nodded. "I want to apologize for being so worked up yesterday. My wife and I are thrilled to not only know that you're okay, but that our son has found his mate."

"It's okay," I said. "I know it's a confusing situation."

"Car is here," Jagger said, interrupting us.

Breaker's father gave me a grateful look before I moved my attention to all the parents. "I want to thank all of you for being so understanding. And even though we have to go back to school, I hope to see you again soon."

"Oh, you will." Celine smiled, coming up to me and giving me a hug. "I plan on holding lots of events coming up. I miss hosting people."

"Sounds great." I squeezed her back. It did sound great....although, maybe not right away. I needed a tiny bit of time to recover from this one.

"Be safe," Leopold repeated. Gage squeezed my waist, a low rumble coming from his throat. It didn't matter that it was his father; my mates didn't like anyone questioning their ability to keep me safe. *I* knew that Leopold wasn't doing that—he was just telling us to be careful overall—but I wasn't positive Gage's dragon got that message.

After saying some quick goodbyes, we made our way into the large car that would take us to the portal, and I couldn't help but reflect on how different this was from my last drive to the portal.

That drive had taken place before I'd remembered Jagger and Breaker. Before I'd discovered I was a dragon. It was crazy to think about.

Per Jagger's request, we made a quick stop at one of the shops downtown on the way. I curled up against Gage's side as Jagger and Breaker went inside, asking him what exactly they were getting. He wouldn't answer me, though, and when they came back out, I scowled when I realized that they were putting their bags in the back with our luggage.

What the heck?

"Why can't I know?" I asked as the door opened and the two of them slid into the vehicle.

"It's a surprise." Breaker winked.

"And how long do I have to wait for this

surprise?" I asked, my voice filled with more than just a little bit of eagerness.

"Till we get back to the dorms," Jagger promised.

Letting out a dramatic huff, I sighed and deflated into the seat. "Fine, fine."

I really didn't mind waiting, though—any surprise from my mates was one worth waiting for.

Chapter Eighteen

Gage Bronzeheart

I could sense a difference in the atmosphere of the academy, a tension that hadn't been there when we left. The headmistress had appeared for all of a few seconds to let us through the portal, disappearing right after we thanked her and leaving us with a group of security who led us to the sector gate.

I knew the others could sense the change too, and Bexley was staring at the security guards in curiosity and concern, trying to get a read on just how serious all of this was. Frustration hit me, hating that she felt the need to worry for even for a damn second. I wanted her beautiful head filled with only good shit, not whatever the academy was dealing with.

"Thank you!" Bexley said to the security

members after they gave us a short goodbye, turning a hard right and disappearing into the sector. When they didn't say anything back, Breaker let out a rumble of annoyance, but considering Bexley was already walking towards the center of campus, I knew she hadn't fully noticed their dismissal.

Which was good, because if she had noticed and then had hurt feelings because of it, I would've had to hunt them down, and considering my cupcake didn't like violence, it didn't put me in the best place overall.

Although, at every turn in this damn place there seemed to be the possibility of conflict—something I had never noticed until Bexley arrived and I'd started assessing each situation for the danger it could pose to her. It was as if the students were actively seeking out confrontations, which if they were predatory shifters was exactly what they were doing. Even now, while there were no classes today—those would start up tomorrow—there were still people gathering in public places outside. One of them brought a sense of déjà vu to the front of my mind from when we had gotten here the first day.

Walker, future Beta to the Clanguard pack.

Although, come to think about it, I hadn't seen him around Fletcher recently. I thought they'd been close, but maybe I was mistaken. I wouldn't blame

Fletcher; Walker was a nuisance in my mind. Then again, that was how I saw a lot of the other male shifters on campus, especially now that Bexley was here.

I would feel a hell of a lot better if I had my mark on her pretty little neck, though...or her mark on me. My gaze narrowed on Jagger. I was happy for my friend, really, but I also was jealous as fuck and craved for Bexley to put her claim on me. My fingers intertwined with hers, needing to touch her.

The past forty-eight hours had been filled with a lot of ups and downs for Bexley. I knew she was far less confused than she'd been in a long time, not only about her past but now, after meeting our parents, her place within the community. Like my parents had predicted, everyone had welcomed her back with open arms.

The past few days had also left me feeling a bit more grounded as well. Of course I felt the need to have as much time with Bexley as possible, but I also recognized that I couldn't occupy all of her attention. I'd known that from the beginning, but it had been a hard pill to swallow at first. For years, I'd had her undivided attention. I was getting used to it now, though, and I couldn't deny the benefit of the extra protection it came with. The multiple eyes looking out for her made me feel far better.

I trusted these men with my life, and now hers.

"You can find somewhere else to hang out," Walker said, his tone somehow both bored and amused. "Fuck off, Erty."

The aggression in his voice had my hackles rising, not only in response to how my dragon felt about it, but because the idea of violence around Bexley made me extremely uncomfortable and protective. I knew my girl didn't feel the same—she may not have liked violence, but she wouldn't walk away in the face of it. In fact, my parents seemed less surprised than I was at her ability to step into violent or aggressive situations without a thought, namely in the effort to protect others.

I knew that wouldn't be the case here, though. There wasn't anyone in need of protection.

My gaze darted to the left, taking stock of the situation. Walker and a few of Fletcher's wolves were relaxing, and Erty, along with some other aquatic shifters, had just approached them, clearly wanting to claim the space for themselves.

"We normally have our class out here, and we need to talk about shit," Erty said matter-of-factly. Unfortunately, aquatic shifters were not only in the minority here, but they suffered within our society in general, constantly overlooked by every group. If Erty didn't look out for his group of shifters, no one would. We did our best within our clan territories to try to mediate it, but most of them lived in the city where they could have their own communities and make their own rules. And because there was a large body of water in the city, a saltwater lake, there was only so much we could do.

I didn't like it, but I would be the first to admit that I hadn't given it as much thought as I probably should have.

"I don't give a fuck," Walker replied. "Fuck off, shark boy."

Bexley came to a hard stop, and I felt her dragon's magic push out and roll over her skin, a flash of black scales and then gold rolling over her jawline and neck. Despite her dragon still being very much part of her, there was a significant change when her magic came to play, and the way she was watching them right now wasn't the way my cupcake normally regarded people.

"Walker is a beta," I said to Bex. "Fletcher's beta, specifically."

"Erty is one the same level as Walker," Breaker agreed. "They'll be—"

I knew he was about to say *fine*, but all of the sudden, Walker said something that caused Erty to lunge forward. I cursed as they crashed into the table and everyone scattered out of the way. Bexley winced as Erty landed a solid punch to Walker's face before the latter managed to dislodge him. The wolf shifter was bristling with anger and looked on the verge of shifting, which meant we needed to get Bexley out of here. I didn't want an adult male were-wolf around her, ever.

"Stop." Bexley's voice wasn't filled with the same magical dominance she'd used before on the girl in the cafeteria, but it was clear as a bell what she wanted. It also drew everyone's attention to her as Erty's eyes flashed with something that almost looked like appreciation. His gaze moved to mine as he took a step back, deferring to Bexley.

Bexley didn't realize just how much power she held, and not only of the magical variety.

"Well, if it isn't our little dragon," Walker drew out, crossing his arms. "Or should we call you *savior* instead?"

"Watch yourself," Jagger warned. I knew Walker meant it disrespectfully, but him calling Bexley anything—more specifically *our* little dragon—had me tightening my hand in hers, attempting to temper my reaction.

"Savior?" Bexley asked, her brows dipping.

"You keep saving all these little pieces of shit. I thought it was just prey, but apparently not," Walker bit out. I'd known the wolf beta for about a year now, and the animosity he was showing towards Bexley was out of character.

Bexley let go of my hand and stepped forward. "This may be an even fight, but I still don't like it. I have no idea why it has to escalate—"

"So a pacifist then," Walker interrupted. "Ridiculous. What type of shifter are you?"

"Walker, I would walk away," I warned, my body rigid with tension from trying to hold back from hurting him.

"So Erty and his fish buddies can take this spot? I don't think so. You don't give a fuck, Gage, you just want to make her happy. So no, I'm not leaving. I'm tired of her shit."

"Tired of what?" Bexley demanded, putting a hand on my chest so I couldn't lunge forward. "What have I done to you, Walker?"

"You're making them think they belong here!" he snarled, pointing at Erty. "The prey shifters, the aquatic shifters. None of them deserve to be here! Now my fucking alpha is mated to some worthless rabbit bitch—"

I shouldn't have been surprised when Bexley disappeared from my side—it was her friend he was talking about, after all—but I was surprised nonetheless. I was even more surprised when she slammed her hand against Walker's chest and vaulted black electricity through him, causing him to jolt like he was being struck by lightning. His agonized cry sounded before he collapsed, unconscious.

Shit.

"Do *not* talk about Rachel like that."

Bexley's voice was filled with true fury like I had never heard before. She stepped back, her breathing uneven and body trembling, Breaker gently leading her away from the wolves and aquatic shifters, who were all staring at her in shock.

Instead of seeing regret in her eyes, which I would have expected, I saw satisfaction. I also saw that her dragon was at the front of her consciousness, her eyes completely black. Her dragon was extremely protective over those she considered in her clan, but I worried that when she calmed down she'd regret what she'd done. We needed to get her out of here before that happened.

"Take him to Fletcher and tell him what happened," I ordered the wolves and then looked towards the aquatic shifters. "Remember what happened today, Erty." Because if any of them tried to challenge Bexley, I would lose my mind.

"We need to go," Jagger urged. I looked down to see Bexley still staring at Walker, her eyes beginning to bleed gold on the edges.

I nodded sharply and picked Bexley up, her arms wrapping around me as she melted against my frame. As we reached our dorm, I felt the moment when Bexley fully came back into herself. A tremble rolled over her as a pained noise left her throat.

"Gage—"

"Almost home," I promised as we reached the elevator and I gently set her down.

"I hurt him. I hurt him really bad," she whispered, tears crowding her eyes. "Why did I do that? How did I do that? I've never used power like that—"

"It's attached to your storm dragon powers..." I trailed off, realizing what her move had probably revealed to all present. I mean, it would become common knowledge soon enough who Bexley was, and more importantly the type of dragon she was, because of the event we held, but the magic she used would also clue people in. Only storm dragons could do what she'd done today.

"I shouldn't have reacted like that," she said, starting to panic. "I need to say something, maybe apologize—"

Breaker shook his head.

"Breaker, I have to—"

"No. You absolutely do not apologize to that piece of shit," Breaker rumbled. "It's okay if you're upset about what you did, although it was a completely natural reaction, but *do not* apologize to him."

"He deserved it," Jagger agreed. I offered both of them curious looks, clearly not having caught the same thing about Walker as they had. Or maybe it was because I was focused on Bexley.

The elevator doors opened, and we stepped into the main room.

"What do you mean?" she asked. "Because he was being a jerk?"

"Sit." Breaker motioned towards the island and started to make tea. I sat next to her and looked at Jagger, who appeared conflicted.

"Think back on what he said," he suggested, and I mentally ran through Walker's words. "He said aquatic shifters and prey shifters don't belong here. He believes they're less than him."

"So do most predatory shifters, it seems," Bexley murmured.

"But Walker is a cousin to the Clanguard family and part of their pack—the future beta," Jagger said.

Ah. Now I got it.

"He wasn't just saying any of that in the heat of the moment," I explained. "He truly believes that. In fact, the entire Clanguard pack is like that, purists who hate anyone that isn't a wolf shifter."

Bexley frowned. "Fletcher doesn't seem like that. Is that why he won't talk about Rachel?"

"I think he's trying to protect her," Breaker said, "although the only way to do that is to take a stand against his own family. He can't bring her home to them; they would eat her alive. Literally."

"What?!"

"Breaker," I chastised, shooting him a dry look.

Breaker shrugged. "I've heard rumors."

"Fates," Bexley groaned. "So I shouldn't feel bad because Walker isn't just a jerk, but like, an actual POS."

"Piece of shit?" Jagger asked at her abbreviation.

"Yes." I chuckled, loving that she still disliked swearing. There was something adorable about the lengths she would go to avoid it.

Bexley's cheeks were pink. "Am I right, though?"

"Yes," Breaker said seriously.

"Has the Clanguard pack always been like this?"

"As long as we can remember," I admitted. "Even growing up, they were a huge issue, constantly trying to start problems with our clans. If I remember correctly, they didn't like the prospect of us having so many storm dragons. They said it left too much potential for a power imbalance or some shit."

"Just wait till they realize the three of us are mated to Bexley, who's both an heir and a storm dragon," Jagger mused. "They'll be calling a meeting with our parents, I can almost guarantee it."

Bexley deflated, running a hand over her face. "I still don't feel good about what I did. Even if he's horrible, I shouldn't have reacted like that."

"You're protective over your friend," I stated. "Plus, on the chance you need to defend yourself, now you know what you are capable of. You know that you aren't defenseless by any means."

"That's true," she murmured, her eyes sparking with energy as she looked at the sky above us, her thoughts drawing elsewhere. "Is it going to storm soon?"

"Tomorrow, probably," Jagger predicted.

"Can...can we fly today then?" she asked softly. "I haven't shifted since the Ioan thing, and I meant to ask if we could when we were at the estate."

"That would have been a great idea," I said, wishing I'd thought of that. But we'd been so caught up on that damn event, you could hardly blame us. "I think we could probably go up for a flight if we just stick to the back of the sector and the mountains there."

"Her energy is all over the place; it's a good idea," Breaker noted. "Plus it will give Jagger and I a moment to go handle the situation with Fletcher, make sure nothing comes of what Walker did. Maybe even talk to Erty."

"I don't want you to have to do cleanup for me," Bexley said, her voice filled with pain. That was hardly what they were proposing, though. They were just trying to present it in a way that seemed less threatening than what it was.

"Not cleanup, a warning," Jagger said.

"Oh." She drew in her bottom lip and nodded. "Okay. Just don't—well, never mind, I don't have a right to say that anymore."

"Bexley." I turned her towards me and examined her face. "Look at me."

She looked up, her eyes filled with guilt.

"Your dragon is going to make you do a lot of stupid shit," I said firmly. "That doesn't mean you will agree with all of it. We understand that you don't like violence, and even if your dragon made you act out in defense of your friend, it doesn't change the way *you* feel about violence, okay? You can still not like it. We understand more than anyone what it feels like to be at odds with your animal side."

Relief filled Bexley's gaze. "You're right." She took in a breath. "Okay, you're totally right."

"Good. Now go get ready."

I watched as she went to Jagger and Breaker, offering both of them a kiss before disappearing into her room. I gave my friends a look, and they nodded, both on the same page as me.

A warning was the least of what Walker deserved, but we would start there. If he escalated it past that, well, then it wouldn't be our fault what followed, would it?

Chapter Nineteen

Bexley Blackforge

Despite what Gage had said, my thoughts weighed heavy as I reflected on what I'd done and how I'd hurt Walker. I didn't think he deserved an apology, per se, especially after realizing how skewed his thought process was, but it didn't mean I felt good about what I'd done. I hadn't even realized what I'd done until moments after, blinded by my dragon's rage. It was an odd sensation that I hadn't fully accepted yet.

As Gage and I walked out onto the bridges to shift, I could tell he was aware that my mind was elsewhere, but instead of trying to pull me into the present, he ran a soothing hand over my back again and again.

"Cupcake, you sure you want to go flying?" he asked softly as we reached the middle of the bridge leading towards Breaker's dorm on the outskirts of the structure.

"Yeah, I need to get out of my head," I said, looking over the edge. "Should we be doing this from the ground?"

"The fall should get you to shift instinctively instead of overthinking it," he explained, "but I'll go down there to catch you in case you don't shift. Then we can try it from there."

"Okay." I nibbled my lip and watched as he vaulted himself over the railing. I leaned over to watch him descend, and when he landed in an extremely agile crouch, I couldn't help but be impressed.

"You've got this," he called up. "Just jump."

"Freaking easy enough for him to say," I grumbled, getting up onto the railing after slipping off my boots.

Inhaling, I looked down at Gage and closed my eyes, trying to pull at that flame at the center of my chest. I wanted to be prepared before I jumped, and I felt emboldened when it came to the front of my consciousness with extreme ease. A boiling sensation rolled over my skin, similar to the one I got when Walker insulted Rachel, except this wasn't anger. This was excitement.

Without a second thought and in a flash of bravery, I jumped off the railing. Like a parachute, I tugged the flame to the front and center to save me from falling.

I shifted.

Energy rolled over my skin, lightning cracked in my ears, and a creature exploded from within me, causing everything to go black for a moment...until I was airborne.

On pure instinct, I soared straight up to avoid a potential crash on the ground, and I couldn't help the pure giddiness and joy that pushed through me because of what I'd accomplished. Moments later a surge of power filled the air as a much larger figure pulled up next to me, bronze scales flashing in the cloudy skies.

Gage.

Of course I'd seen him shift before, but in the sky he was absolutely magnificent. His dark eyes met mine, and when he turned a sharp left, I didn't question it. I just followed him, his massive wingspan filling the air in front of me.

I sped forward in an effort to keep up, accidentally passing him in a sprint of energy. A rumble left him, but I couldn't contain the excited sound that left my throat, realizing just how powerful I was. How fast and strong I had the potential to be.

The energy released from the action also went a

long way to make me feel better, my body pulsing with a power that pulled me from my troubled thoughts. My only focus was on flying.

As if knowing it was helping, Gage began to lead me through the skies, allowing me to race him at times and other times going through a series of twists and turns that felt a lot like an obstacle course. I hadn't even realized how long we'd been flying until the skies began to darken and Gage soared towards a familiar cave, the one that I'd flown to on my first flight here a few days ago.

I remembered that now. I also remembered the three of them calming me down and trying to convince me to shift back before I passed out.

When we landed in the cave, I immediately shifted back and collapsed onto the stone with a laugh. My muscles were so freaking sore, and when I rolled on my back, my eyes widened, realizing that Gage *hadn't* shifted back.

His dragon was staring down at me, his snout only inches away from my face. Lifting a hand, I ran my fingers across his scales, eliciting a low rumble that had my skin prickling. Except for once or twice, I don't think I'd ever been this close to his shifted form.

"Gage," I whispered, and it was as if the sound of his name had called his human side to the forefront.

He shifted immediately, and I gasped as he landed nearly on top of me, pinning me to the ground but still keeping his weight off me. His dragon wasn't gone, though—not completely. His magic was still riding him, dangerously close to the surface. There was a darkness to his gaze that I wasn't used to seeing until recently, and it made everything feel far more serious.

"You are so beautiful," he said, his voice rough. He leaned closer, his lips brushing mine. "Seeing you in the sky like that... Fates, you're magnificent, cupcake."

My cheeks exploded with heat as desire rolled through me. I pressed my thighs together as his eyes turned pure bronze, clearly able to tell how his words were affecting me.

"I loved flying with you," I admitted breathlessly.

"My dragon loved it as much as I did," he growled softly. "That's why he wouldn't let me shift back right away—he wanted you to see him, cocky bastard."

"You are amazing, and so is your dragon."

He nipped my lip, clearly liking the compliment. "He's upset you marked Jagger first. Jealous, really." He chuckled softly, a dark note to his voice.

"And how do you feel?" I asked, my skin prickling with the awareness that something was different

251

about Gage right now, his energy far more predatory than normal. I wasn't worried about his answer or his reaction to what happened with Jagger—or at least I hadn't been—but now his words made me wonder if it was bothering him more than he let on.

"I want you to mark me, cupcake, and even more so, I want to cover you in my marks. I've always wanted that, but I've waited this long, and I plan to wait as long as necessary. I would never want you to feel pressured."

I believed him, but I could also see the pain associated with his words, how much he needed me and how much he'd been holding back.

"What if I don't want you to wait anymore?" I whispered, trying to be bold as heat infused every square inch of my skin.

Gage's gaze darkened. "I can't mark you, cupcake. Not here. I wouldn't be able to control myself."

"And if I didn't want you to control yourself?"

He stilled, trembling with restraint as he lowered himself further against me. I parted my thighs for him, liking the feeling of his weight between my legs.

Gage let out a deep groan. "I can't take you, not here. I can't."

"Why not?"

"It needs to be perfect, I—"

"It already is." I ran my fingers up his jaw and into his hair. "It's always perfect with you. I don't care where we are, Gage. I just want you."

His gaze regarded mine for a long second before something snapped free. "Fuck it."

I moaned as his lips met mine in a hot, demanding kiss. My legs wrapped around his hips as my fingers dug into his hair, securing him to me. It seemed to fuel him, and when he rolled us so that I was on top of him, I gasped at just how hard he was underneath me. Gage was big, I knew that, but feeling him so directly between my legs caused my body to break into a fiery inferno.

"Sweater off," he demanded.

He groaned as I immediately complied with his command, slipping my sweater over my head, his fingers running over my skin as I tossed it to the side and began to pull at his shirt. He sat up, yanking the offensive garment off his body, allowing my hands to greedily run over his warm skin. When he flipped us again, making sure to lay me on top of our discarded clothes, I could see that his control and restraint were about to truly break. There was a tension to him as he looked over me, his breathing rough.

"Are you sure, cupcake? I'm barely hanging on."

"Yes," I gasped. "Please, Gage." My words sounded as needy as I felt, and I held my breath as I waited for him to give in. This wasn't an option anymore. Right now it felt like my body was on fire with need for him.

I exhaled in relief as he undid my jeans and slid them down my legs. He regarded me almost reverently as each inch of skin was exposed, and I opened my legs further for him, leaning up to pull him to me.

He placed a palm on my hip, effectively halting the action. "Stay just like that, cupcake. I've been wanting to look at you like this for a long time now, and I plan on taking my fill."

I tried to not move, but I could barely stay still, my skin tingling with the need for his touch. As if knowing, his fingers moved to the lace of my panties and he snapped the sides, tossing them. His eyes closed and his nostrils flared as he scented me, and my cheeks turned bright red...until his mouth met my center.

"Gage!" I cried as his tongue ran over my wet heat, my body so worked up that I nearly came right then. His hands tightened on my thighs as he continued to work and tease my body, my center growing even more wet as he held my climax right out of reach.

"Need to get you ready," he rasped. "Fuck, you taste good."

"I need to come," I whimpered.

"You'll come on my cock then," he growled, sliding two fingers inside of me. The action nearly had my eyes rolling into the back of my head as he pumped his fingers in and out of me, my body adjusting to the size of his digits.

His voice was filled with a primal roughness that almost made it hard to understand him. "Fuck, you are so tight. So tight. I have no idea how I'm going to fit inside of you, cupcake."

"Please, Gage." I nearly cried with how frustrated I was, my entire body trembling.

"I don't want to hurt you."

"Please," I begged again as his lips brushed against my neck. I was going crazy, my body mindlessly urging for *more*.

Pulling his fingers out, he brought them to his mouth and licked them clean. His other hand worked to unbuckle his pants, releasing his erection. *Holy fates.* Gage was right—how was he going to fit inside of me?

My eyes moved back up to his, which were shining with pure need and adoration. It was a toxic and amazing combination that made me want him that much more, dissolving my worries.

"You think you can fit all of me?"

"Yes," I whispered, and when his cock slid over

my slick entrance, my body broke into a heated flush, the cool air only increasing the sensation.

"Let's see, cupcake. Let's see how much this little pussy can fit."

As he began to slide in, I gasped at the pleasurable intrusion. Gage leaned down before he was fully seated, kissing my lips and whispering the words I'd been needing to hear from him forever. "I love you, cupcake. I fucking love you."

Then he thrust inside of me. His massive length and his words had the entire world exploding in blazing heat, the pain of him invading my body absolutely nothing compared to the raw, primal connection soaring through me, the fullness making me feel like I was complete. Like he was finally home where he needed to be. Tears streamed down my face at the rightness.

"Fuck," he groaned, his words almost slurred. "I'm so sorry. I'll make it better."

"You feel so good," I whispered, surprise and then a lethal heat filling his expression. "You feel s-so good. I need you to move, though. You're so big."

His cock pulsed at that, and he grunted and pulled back just slightly before pushing forward, my gaze moving down to where we were joined. There was blood there, and the proof of him taking me for the first time had me tightening around him further, loving the base connection it represented. I gripped his shoulders, moaning his name at the sensation of him filling me once again.

"I love you," I whimpered.

My words seemed to break something inside of him. He pulled back and pushed back in, harder this time, beginning to pump in and out of me at a deep, intense pace. My nails dug into his back as I tightened my legs around him, loving the feeling of him lodging himself so deeply inside of me. I cried out his name as he slammed into me, my entire body shuddering in relief and an electric shock going right to my clit.

"Mark me," he growled against my lips. "Mark me while I drill inside of you, cupcake."

He didn't have to ask twice. My lips found his throat, and I bit down eagerly, his groan of my name and the way his cock pulsed making me think he'd come inside of me. That thought alone, along with the satisfaction of his bronze threads of magic intertwining with my obsidian ones, had a small climax rolling over me as he pulled back and began to do exactly as he said—drill into me.

The scent of blood from my mark and him taking my virginity filled the air as my magic caused electricity to crack through the space. While I could feel the cave floor scratching my back, I didn't care. I loved the feeling of him taking me so roughly, of him needing me so much that he couldn't wait.

"Gage!" I screamed as he hit so deeply that white-hot points of pleasure had me nearly climaxing around his cock. *Holy fates.* This felt so incredible, but I needed to come. I felt dizzy with need.

His pace grew faster and less even as the sound of him pounding in and out of me filled the cave, the erotic noise causing me to only grow closer and closer to a climax I knew that would absolutely destroy me. When his lips drew down my jaw and to my throat, I arched against his mouth, wanting his teeth to slice into my skin.

"I'm going to come inside you, Bex," he groaned. "I'm going to fill you up with so much cum it'll stay between your thighs all day."

Holy shit. I wanted that. I wanted that so much.

More than anything, though, I wanted his mark. When my nails dug into his back, he bit my throat, causing me to absolutely detonate. A storm suddenly exploded out of me, pure euphoria filling my senses as electricity and thunder sounded outside and echoed through the cave. I cried out as our bond solidified, the twisted rope of our magic threads now coated in bronze. Unbreakable. Eternal.

When he slammed into me one last time, roaring

out my name, I felt his hot release fill me. I whimpered at the feeling, and when he held himself inside of me, I melted into the ground, unable to keep my eyes open. Everything around me was hazy and filled with a euphoric light that caused my head to spin.

I pouted as Gage finally pulled back, and when my eyes opened, I found him staring at our combined release, his cock still hard as he ran the tip over my slit.

"Gage," I whispered, leaning up on my elbows to watch him push some of his cum back inside of me. His eyes languidly rose to meet mine as he did it again, and the action had something inside of me smoldering as Gage let out a noise that was completely inhuman.

When his lips met mine, I smoothed my hands over his back, and the scent of blood filled the air. I pulled back, finding my hands coated in blood.

"What the—"

"Your claws," he said with a hint of pride. "You shifted slightly, and your claws marked my back."

"And you're okay with that?" I asked, embarrassed that I'd lost control enough to hurt him.

"Feel free to do it again," he growled, nipping my lip. "Mark me any way you want, as many times as you want, because I want my marks all over you too, cupcake."

"I love you," I whispered, a softer smile flashing on his lips as he whispered it back. Relaxing back into the ground, I felt him slide his cum back inside of me once more before he slid my jeans back on for me.

"I'm so tired," I whispered.

"You flew and got fucked—now you need food," Gage said softly, although there was a bit of amusement to his voice.

"Right." I sighed happily, my eyes heavy. "Maybe I'll just close my eyes for a minute..."

I curled into Gage's chest, trusting him to get us back home.

Chapter Twenty

Bexley Blackforge

O ne minute I was sleeping in Gage's arms, trusting that he would get me back to the dorms, and the next I was waking up in bed surrounded by all my mates. Before I even opened my eyes, a sleepy, satisfied smile filled my face. I hadn't had a moment to consider it, but now that I was in bed with them, any fears of them being upset about what had happened between Gage and me slipped away. I shouldn't have been surprised, but when Breaker's arm tightened around me, grumbling about something under his breath, I let out a happy sigh.

"Cupcake." Gage's voice was soft as it ran over my ears. My eyes opened to find him standing next to the bed, looking down at me with so much warmth it made my toes curl. Jagger was underneath my head, sleeping. I knew that ever since the Ioan thing, they switched off keeping watch at night, so I had to assume that was what Gage was doing up.

"Morning," I whispered.

"I'm going to run out to talk to our professors," Gage said, moving my hair out of my face. "Your morning class should be okay, but there's a storm rolling in, so after that we're going to come back to the dorms."

"Because the storms increase our power, right?" I was more than a bit sleepy right now, so it was possible I was wrong, but I didn't think so...

A warm light filled his gaze. "I love that you said *our* power. But yeah, you're right. It makes them act fucking crazy, so I'm going to tell our professors and give them a warning that we may not be in class, just in case."

"Sounds good," I murmured, yawning as my eyes closed once more.

I drifted in and out of sleep, happily curled up between Jagger and Breaker, and it was only the sound of rain on the roof and the absence of two warm bodies in bed that finally pulled me from my slumber. Letting out a big yawn, I stretched, groaning at how good it felt. I wouldn't lie, I was still a bit sore from both the flight and Gage, but overall I felt amazing.

"Mo chuisle." Breaker was suddenly next to me, and I offered him a sleepy smile.

"Hey, you," I whispered, sitting up fully—which is when I saw *them.* Them being the three stuffed dragons in the center of the bed, each in different shades of red, blue, and green. They were beautiful, and I didn't even bother trying to contain the urge to snap them up into my arms as Breaker chuckled. I held them to my chest and looked up at him in surprise.

"What are these? They are freakin' adorable." And would absolutely fit with my other three dragons, although they were slightly smaller than them, which made it that much cuter.

Breaker let out an amused hum and sat on the edge of the bed. "What we got yesterday. We figured if Gage got to say he had children with you—"

"We could also," Jagger finished for him as he appeared with a mug of what smelled like peppermint coffee.

"I love that." I slipped out of bed and went to the chair that already held the other three dragons, placing a smaller dragon in front of each so they were like a happy little family. I turned with realization. "Wait, now I need one that looks like me. The three from Gage look like the three of you, and then if these are our kids..."

"Then we need one of you," Breaker agreed, and despite the light tone of the conversation, I could see a rolling darkness in his gaze, mixed with heat. I think Breaker liked the direction of this conversation a lot, and I couldn't lie...I did as well.

"We can make that happen," Jagger said, handing me the coffee and kissing the top of my head. "But before we do that, we need to get you some breakfast."

"What about class?" I looked up at the stormy skies. "Crap, did I miss it? I'm never going to make it to this freakin' class at this rate."

"You didn't miss it," Jagger promised. "It's just starting to storm, so we aren't going."

"Oh." I deflated. "Is it okay for us to go to breakfast then?"

"Should be—most students will already be going to class by the time we get there."

I nodded and looked down at my stuffed animals before going up on my toes and giving Jagger a kiss. I then rounded the room and did the same to Breaker. "You both are amazing," I said softly.

Breaker chuckled. "Make sure to mention that to Gage—he's been walking around like he's king of the world this morning."

Jagger wrapped an arm around me from behind and tucked a piece of hair behind my ear. "I suppose I can't blame him. I'd feel the same way if I had the honor of being with Bexley."

Oh my fates.

My skin broke out into shivers as I tilted my head back to look at him, and Breaker let out a hum of agreement. The way the two of them were looking at me was enough to make my knees weak, and if it wasn't for the sound of the elevator door opening... Well, I wasn't sure what I would do. I knew what my body wanted, but I wasn't positive I was ready for that.

"Here he comes," Jagger grunted, and I let out a small giggle at his disappointment at being interrupted.

"Cupcake, you're up. Good," Gage said as he entered my bedroom. His eyes immediately went to me, warmth infusing them as he smiled. It was a reckless and gorgeous look that had me feeling momentarily breathless.

Then he looked at the other two and scowled. "If either of you try to cover my scent on her, I'll kill you."

I blinked in surprise as Jagger laughed—literally laughed—thoroughly amused. I was confused for a minute, but then Breaker's fingers smoothed right over my throat, narrowly avoiding my new mating mark.

"Would never even consider it, buddy," Breaker said, but it didn't stop Gage from tracking his every movement. Did he not want him to touch my mating mark? I felt like that was kind of unavoidable.

"Wait, I love having all of your scents on me," I said. Gage looked like he was freaking pouting, but there was a lightness to him today, one that seemed to fill the entire room with an electric energy.

"He'll be fine, his dragon just needs twenty-four hours," Jagger said, still sounding amused and unbothered by the notion.

"Until then, he's going to be weird," Breaker confirmed.

"We need to get her breakfast," Gage said, continuing as if they hadn't said anything, "I'm worried you haven't eaten yet. We should just go now."

"I have to brush my teeth," I said as I stepped from between them, holding my coffee to my nose as I passed Gage. I lightly kissed his cheek, making a rumble escape his throat, and I disappeared into the main room and towards the bathroom.

I swear I heard Breaker say something about Gage acting like a psycho, but it was muffled when I closed the bathroom door. My eyes widened at the reflection that greeted me in the mirror. What the heck?

The first thing I noticed was that I looked like a hot mess. Enough so that I turned on the shower because my hair looked like a rat's nest, tangled in some spots and pressed flat in others. My clothes were messy and wrinkled, though I was thankful that Gage had changed me into something more comfortable once we got home. I still didn't know how he'd done that...I would have to ask.

The second thing I noticed was the mark on my neck. There was a bite mark, of course, but in the center of the mark was a patch of bronze scales. They were faint and seemed to almost blend into my skin, but I knew I wasn't imagining them as I watched them sparkle beneath the bathroom vanity lights. Had my marks on Gage and Jagger done the same?

Stepping out of the bathroom, I found Jagger in the kitchen. I walked up to him and pulled down the collar of his sweater without explanation. My bite was still there, but no scales. Walking over to Gage, who was watching me with interest—I wasn't sure where Breaker had disappeared to—I turned his neck and found a patch of black scales.

"Well, that answers that." I made a happy noise and went back towards the bathroom.

"Wait, what?" Gage asked.

"She's trying to figure out when the scales appear on the mating marks," Jagger said, having put it together. He kissed the side of my head in passing, explaining, "It happens when we've both marked one another."

"Makes sense." I nodded and looked down at my mark on him, my dragon not liking that it wasn't a completely solidified bond.

"In the shower, now," Jagger rumbled. "I can see where your thoughts are going, little treasure."

I couldn't help my small smile as I made an amused noise and slipped into the bathroom, closing the door.

After taking a long, relaxing shower, massaging the conditioner into my hair and making sure to give my muscles a good stretch, I turned off the water and stepped out, wrapping myself in a robe. I took the time to blow-dry my hair before braiding it into two long french braids. I didn't bother with makeup, and when I stepped out into the main room, only Gage was there, stretched out on the couch with his eyes closed. It seemed the other two were getting dressed, so I slipped into my bedroom and did the same.

I went with leggings and an oversized sweater, figuring I could change into something even comfier when we got back here. Pulling on rain boots and a windbreaker, I tugged a hat on over my braids and stepped back out, my stomach rumbling. Right then, Breaker appeared and looked over me, his eyes flashing with heat and affection.

"You look adorable, Bex."

"I do?" I looked down at myself curiously.

"It's the braids," Gage said, sitting up.

"Although now I can only think about pulling them," Breaker said as he approached my side, his hand tugging on my braid. Turning towards him, I watched as he wrapped the braid around his fist and pulled just a little bit. My skin broke into shivers as his eyes snapped to mine, a smirk tugging at his lips.

"Yeah, I like these," he whispered, kissing my forehead before pulling back. "Alright, let's head out."

I nearly pouted, my body in absolute disagreement with leaving the dorm when it seemed Breaker was interested in more fun stuff...

"I'm actually a bit hungry," Jagger agreed, my dragon instantly hyper-focused on the fact that our mate wanted something. As we walked towards the elevator and stepped in, the question from before popped into my head.

"Wait, Gage, how did we get back last night?"

"He flew with you on his back," Breaker growled,

his tone disapproving. Jagger made a sound of agreement as Gage squeezed my hand.

"You were perfectly safe. Our magic provides protection for anyone riding us," he explained easily.

"Oh, okay," I said as we stepped out of the elevator. Breaker was instantly glued to my side, opening an umbrella and holding it over my head. The others pulled up the hoods of their jackets, and I found myself wanting to find an umbrella for them also, but then we were walking out into the wind and rain.

Thunder cracked overhead, and exhilaration ran over my skin as lightning flashed. It wasn't a full storm yet, but I could tell it was building, a feeling that my magic confirmed. I wasn't sure if we could shift during storms... I mean, I knew we could, but I wasn't sure if it was a good idea if we affected students so much. Then again, if we were in the back of the sector...

When we reached the main academic building, Breaker closed the umbrella, and I shook off my jacket to get any extra rain drops off me. I was distracted enough that when I looked up, I hadn't realized that there were a lot more students around than I would have expected...and they were all staring.

That alone wouldn't have been that surprising, but it was pointedly directed at me, and I didn't understand why. It was clear my mates caught on also because they moved closer as we walked towards the dining hall, finding it moderately empty. I could hear the murmurs and whispers from the hallway behind us, though, making me feel self-conscious.

"Do we think they know?" I asked softly. "Like about the event—do you think the news has gotten around?"

"Probably," Gage admitted. "Paired with what happened yesterday with Walker... Yeah, it's entirely possible."

"Fletcher said he understood," Breaker said, "but that doesn't mean everyone else did."

"Or maybe it's just because of the Walker thing. I mean, you knocked a beta unconscious," Jagger pointed out, making me wince at the memory.

When we reached a table, Breaker sat and pulled me onto his knee as the other two went to grab food. My thoughts were pulled in a million directions, like all the eyes I felt on me.

"I hate to think it's about Walker," I said, leaning into him. I didn't want others to ever think I would use my magic to hurt them. He pressed a comforting kiss to my shoulder, but before he could say anything, the sound of approaching footsteps drew both of our gazes.

Diane.

Except the normal distrust in her gaze was gone, and instead there was a smile on her face—an authentic one. She grabbed a chair and sat down at our table, propping up her chin on her hand. "Tell me it's true, Bex. Tell me that you knocked Walker on his ass."

"I mean, it didn't go exactly—"

"Yes," Breaker answered. "She did. But it was because Walker was insulting her friend as well as talking about how certain shifters shouldn't go to the academy."

I knew that he hadn't needed to tell Diane all that, but he'd summed it up so efficiently, and it sounded a lot better when he said it like that... Although I still felt weird about it.

"Good," Diane said. "I'm glad you did. He's a total creep. Good on you."

"Is that why everyone is staring?" I asked her, noticing that there were even more eyes on us now.

"Partly," she said before adding, "Plus word got out that you're some lost dragon heir to a clan that used to be in the rogue lands—that sound right? I have no idea, nor do I care. Not my business, nor should it matter to anyone who lives in the city. But yeah, both things are circulating, so that would explain it."

"Thanks," I breathed out. "Yeah, both are true."

"Sweet. Thanks for the Walker thing—he needed to be brought down a peg." Then she was gone before I even had a chance to say anything back. I swear, people were always walking away from me.

Looking over the expressions of students staring at us, I found there wasn't nearly the same level of happiness that Diane had exhibited. Instead there was anger, mistrust, and confusion, none of which were good in my mind. I ran a hand over my face, wondering how I was going to handle this.

"Don't focus too much on them. Our magic is amping their emotions up as well, so if someone would normally be upset about what you did to Walker, today they will be angry—which is why we aren't going to class," he explained quietly.

"That's frustrating." But it did make me feel moderately better.

When thunder boomed in the sky, far closer this time, I felt a surge in my magic. It was like the sound had directly fueled it, injecting me with a shot of adrenaline. It was addicting.

"Hey, Breaker?" I murmured, seeing the others were walking back with our food. "Can we grab our breakfast to go?" I didn't want to risk anyone else coming up to us right now. If he was right, then people wouldn't be exactly in a good frame of mind to hear my side of the story.

"Absolutely," Breaker said, standing us up. "I have a feeling the storm is about to get pretty bad."

I knew he was talking about the weather...but it felt like so much more than that.

Chapter Twenty-One

Bexley Blackforge

After eating breakfast in the dorms together and watching the storm, it lightened up just enough that I could step outside, so I decided to get some fresh air. At first I could tell my mates were worried, but after I bundled up and said I would be staying right in the area of our dorm, they seemed to understand.

I also knew that Breaker was standing outside on the bridges right now, keeping an eye on our surroundings so I could walk the space without fear of danger. It was beyond sweet and honestly needed right now since my headspace was cluttered. My thoughts bounced between the conversation in the cafeteria, what others knew about me now, and even what a garden would look like here.

I felt frazzled and a bit out of place.

Ungrounded. Letting out a huff of frustration, I closed my eyes and tried to focus on the one thing I knew I needed to figure out for sure. *What name was said in that memory.* Tucking my hands into the pockets of my jacket, I squeezed my eyes shut tighter and tried to focus on the clouded mirror of my memories.

Wanting to clear the fogginess from it, I began to just try to wipe it away, although it wasn't doing much good. At least I thought it wasn't...

"Mom!" I called, my voice echoing through her suite as I searched for her. When I heard her call my name back, I walked towards her closet and stepped into a space that I'd always found somewhat magical. It was filled with so many dresses in different colors, fabrics, and levels of glitter. I absolutely loved it.

My mom looked up at me from where she was searching through a box on the ground and offered me an affectionate smile. "You finally woke up! I was worried you were going to sleep all day."

I yawned, my body clearly trying to betray how tired I still was. "I didn't expect yesterday to make me so sleepy."

"Well, it was your first time training," she reasoned, "and you didn't exactly pick easy sparring

partners. Breaker, Gage, and Jagger may be close to your age, but they've all been in lessons since they were six or seven."

"I should've done the same," I said, scowling. I didn't like fighting at all, even if it was just pretend fighting, but my friends did, and they were good at it, so I felt like it was something I should enjoy as well.

"No, you should have focused on what you enjoyed, which was crafting and drawing. Fighting is important, but only if you want to do it. As a dragon, you have natural defenses you can always lean on," she pointed out, folding something and putting the box away.

"You can fight," I countered, putting my hands on my hips.

"I enjoy fighting. It's fun to kick your dad's butt," she said with a laugh before standing and leading me out of her closet. "But if I didn't enjoy it, I wouldn't do it."

"I need to learn how to kick their butts," I said, making my mom laugh again as we sat down on the couch in the little living room section of her suite. I curled up on the space next to her as she turned on the television.

"Why is that?" she asked finally, running her hands through my hair and starting to braid it, my eyes on the movie.

"Because they think they're super strong and keep telling me about it." I rolled my eyes. *"And I want them to know I'm super strong as well."*

"Oh, I think they know how strong you are," my mom said knowingly. *"Besides, strength comes in all forms, honey. Don't ever forget that."*

Her words echoed in my head as I was released from the memory, and a rush of emotions pulsed through my chest, my eyes pricking as other scenes flashed in front of my closed eyes. Ones of my mom and I spending time together, traveling together, poking fun at my dad. I could remember how in love the two of them were and how I found myself hoping that one day I would find someone who cared for and loved me as much as they loved each other. Tears leaked down my face as I realized just how important our little family was to my parents, how it was truly their everything.

"Jericho, we need to leave," my mom said as we entered my dad's office. We were going into the city to see one of my favorite plays, and I'd been looking forward to it all month, especially since we didn't go into the city very often.

"Almost ready." My father stood, and my gaze darted to the men around him, all looking a bit frustrated at his words. "Gentlemen, we will have to finish this later—I have big plans tonight."

"Sir," one of them started, but darkness flashed across my dad's face as he silenced the man with a single lift of his hand.

"I have plans. Please leave."

As they stood and left, I felt a momentary surge of guilt, my lips dipping into a slight frown. I knew this was for my tenth birthday, but if he had important work to do...

"They're ridiculous," my mom said.

"If you have to work—"

My dad appeared in front of me and crouched down, squeezing my hand. "No amount of work is as important as you, Bexley."

I felt relief at his words, nodding.

"Plus, anything that can be done today can also be done tomorrow. The same can't always be said about important moments like this."

It was clear now that it was that simple in my parents' eyes—family always came first.

I couldn't help but wonder if that was the reason my parents had enemies. I needed to know. I needed to know who had taken all of that away from me, who had ripped such a perfect life from my hands. Hot tears continued to trek down my face as I sat down on the damp ground and buried my head against my knees, forcing myself to focus on the other memory. To focus on what Rebecca had said.

But no matter how hard I pushed, to the point that my eyes began to hurt from squeezing them so tightly, I just couldn't make out her words. A heavy surge of disappointment pushed through me, and I felt a sense of deep, immense loss now that memories of my parents were trickling in.

Not just them, though.

As I let go of the concept of remembering what Rebecca had said, my body sagging in defeat, I decided instead to focus on other memories right on the edge of my consciousness. Happier ones. Ones that included my mates, who had been my best friends for years, and like a key to a lock, those memories began to flood in as well. A vibrant one filled with smiles stood out to me.

"I think we should go," I whispered, my focus on the lake up ahead. *"The parents aren't paying attention, and think how surprised Jagger and Gage would be."*

We were crouched in the bushes, but Breaker's

height was drastically different from my own, making it nearly impossible for him to hide. Right now we were fairly concealed, but I knew that Gage and Jagger would be looking for us—which is why we needed to get to the boat before they thought of it.

"I feel like we're breaking the rules of tag if we get on a boat and go to the middle of the lake," Breaker mused.

"No." I shook my head. "We're totally not."

"Bexley!" Gage's voice rang out, causing both Breaker and I to look at each other in panic. I could hear two pairs of footsteps coming—

"Let's do it," he murmured, putting his fingers up to count to three. When the last finger rose, we sprinted towards the shore. I wasn't nearly as fast as him, but from the moment we broke from the bushes, Gage and Jagger caught sight of us. I let out a giggle, screaming as they ran towards us. We'd nearly reached the boat to escape when Jagger grabbed me around the waist.

"No!" I wailed in defeat, trying to push out of his arms.

"Shit," Jagger swore, and before I knew it, both of us fell into the lake, the cold water like an electric shock. I slipped underneath the surface, and when Jagger's hand grabbed my arm and tugged, I broke back up and sucked in oxygen.

A snort broke from my lips at the sight of a drenched Jagger, and when I looked up and saw Gage and Breaker staring at us in shock, I laughed even more. All I could manage was an 'oops' before our parents got there, looking surprised more than anything.

I still couldn't manage to stop laughing, though, and soon my friends joined in.

That happiness, that level of joy, seemed to be a consistent theme throughout the memories, and while I had been blessed by the fates to have had the Bronzehearts and a peaceful, happy childhood, there was loss associated with regaining these memories. The clans had truly been as close as family, and when I lost my parents, when everyone thought I'd died, I lost far more than my memories—I lost everyone.

But that didn't have to be the case anymore.

We could have that back; we just needed to remove the threat of not knowing who had caused the problem in the first place.

"Shit, Bex, are you okay?" Breaker's voice had my eyes snapping open as I was lifted from the ground and into his arms. Instinctively, I wrapped my arms around him and buried my nose against his throat, tears tracking down my face. I nodded, but before I knew it, he had carried us to the shelter of a copse of trees as the rain started to come down once again.

As I lifted my head up from where he had me pinned to the tree, he cupped my jaw and looked over me in concern. "What's wrong?"

Words poured out of me as I told him everything I could remember. Obviously not in extreme detail, but I recounted as many instances as I could of my parents and of us, my voice shaky as I finally said, "We had so much. I was surrounded by so much love, and it was just ripped away, Breaker. Someone took it from us."

Breaker's gaze was filled with pain as he pressed his forehead to mine. "We're going to figure out who it was that did that. Maybe not today, but soon. We won't let it go unpunished, Bexley, I promise you that."

I believed him. More so, the thought of my mates punishing whoever was responsible didn't bother me. If someone was willing to tear apart my family, I had no urge to protect them.

"But even with everything that happened, you are surrounded by love," Breaker reminded me. "You are loved by our families and by us. Remember that, no matter what, you will always have that."

"By you?" I whispered.

"Yes, by me," he growled softly, pressing his lips against mine. "You are all I've thought about since I lost you, and now that you're getting your memories back, I hope you know that there is no way I *can't* love you, Bexley. You are my entire world, *mo chuisle*. My very pulse."

Happy tears trekked down my face as I cupped his jaw. "I love you, Breaker. I know I don't have everything back, but even without every memory, I'm in love with you."

Breaker's kiss was soft and exploratory as he whispered the words back again, causing my toes to curl at the sweet taste that rolled over my lips. I wanted so much of Breaker, but what I wanted more than anything right now was to mark him.

"Breaker." I pulled back and spoke softly, trying to be bold despite being nervous. "Can I... Can I mark you?"

"Fuck," he rumbled. He was bent over me, filling my entire space. "You never need to ask that. I want everyone to know I'm yours."

His words caused an elated shiver to roll over my skin as I trailed my kisses from his lips down his jaw. My teeth pulsed with the need to mark him, to claim him as my mate, and I didn't hesitate when I reached his throat.

I bit down hard, and that familiar magic, my obsidian threads, created a bonded rope with his own gold magic as they wrapped around one another. Breaker let out a feral sound from the back of his throat as I finally released his skin and pulled back, a small smile playing at my lips.

When he kissed me, I could taste his blood mixed with our kiss, and it seemed to fuel something inside of me, lighting a dangerous fire that I knew would never go away. I would always want my mates.

Breaker pulled back and groaned. "Fuck, we need to stop."

"Why?" I whispered, trying not to pout.

"Because I'm going to end up fucking you against this tree, and I know you're probably sore right now, so we need to get your little ass inside."

I wanted to tell him no. I wanted to tell him that with how much he was turning me on, I would be totally fine, but I hesitated for just a moment too long. He offered me a knowing look, and this time I did pout, slumping in his arms as he picked me up easily. Breaker chuckled as he secured his hold on me, his large hands cupping my butt.

"Fine," I grumbled. "I may be a bit sore."

"That's what I thought," he murmured, sounding amused. I flushed, loving and hating how easily he seemed to be able to talk about what Gage and I had done. I needed to bolster some confidence to be able to talk about it that openly.

As we reached the elevators, Jagger appeared, exhaling in relief when he saw us. I didn't understand why until he said, "Clanguard wants to talk to us. We just got notice that he'll be here soon."

Based on their reactions, I was guessing it wasn't a good thing.

Chapter Twenty-Two

Bexley Blackforge

I wasn't normally one to pace, but I couldn't help but nervously walk between the couch and the balcony doors. Back and forth, back and forth. *Totally* not pacing. I couldn't help it though. My instincts told me that Professor Clanguard wasn't coming for a friendly visit.

I knew I wasn't the only one who felt that way either, because Gage was sitting quietly in a chair nearby, his gaze on me but completely silent. Jagger was leaning against the doorway of my bedroom, his brow furrowed. I knew he didn't like the idea of Clanguard coming into my dorm because he'd mentioned it twice now, but it seemed we didn't have much of a choice. Breaker seemed bothered by it as well, but his attention was focused on making tea for me as he tried to keep his hands as busy as possible.

When a buzzing noise sounded, Jagger walked to the elevator and pressed a button I hadn't even known existed until now, clearly put there to allow us to 'buzz' people up so that not just anyone could come into our dorms.

I froze up as I watched the elevator door open, Professor Clanguard walking through and shaking the rain from his hair onto the floor of my dorm. The idea of his scent lingering in my dorm bothered me, and I had a feeling it was the reason Jagger's scowl deepened.

"Good." He nodded sharply after looking around the space. "All of you are here."

"What's the meaning of this?" Gage demanded. "Why couldn't we just meet in your office or at your house again? I don't like you coming to her house."

Clanguard's gaze turned apologetic. "And for that I apologize, especially to you, Bexley. If I thought this was a conversation better had at either of those locations, I would have chosen that. But my office isn't private enough, and Rachel is taking a nap at my house."

At that, a genuine smile broke through my nerves. "I love that you're so open about being her mate."

Clanguard's gaze filled with warmth. "And I appreciate you being a good friend to her. I have it a lot easier than my brother. I don't owe my family anything—I broke away from them years ago—so I'm free to have whatever mate I want. Fletch is far from being in the same position."

"Is that why he doesn't spend a lot of time with her in public?" I asked softly. "I can tell it bothers her."

Clanguard nodded, letting out a long exhale. "Unfortunately, her safety and my family's involvement are drastically intertwined, so for the moment, I understand why he's acting the way he is—even if I think it's bullshit."

I didn't like it, but it made sense. Rachel's safety came first. It was then that I realized my mates were staring at him blankly, clearly not nearly as interested in Professor Clanguard's mate situation as I was.

"Right," Professor Clanguard said, seeming to catch on. "Let me get to the point so I can get out of here. The combination of all your magic in one room is not very pleasant, so I'll try to make this as brief as possible."

I knew he didn't mean it offensively, but I couldn't help but feel bad. I didn't want anyone to have issues being around us, even if it was unavoidable. I also never wanted to make anyone uncomfortable, and I could see the tension running through his frame, telling me he was exactly that. Uncomfortable.

"Alright," Jagger said, prompting him.

"Your event at the Bronzehearts immediately set forth the news that Bexley was the lost and thought-to-be dead heir to the Flash Clan," he said, looking to me for confirmation. I nodded, and he continued. "Because of that, and the knowledge that she is mate to the three of you, there are families, specifically my own, that are unhappy about that imbalance of power and want to confirm for a fact that Bexley is who everyone says she is."

"Fuck them," Breaker growled. "They have no right to question anything."

"Unfortunately, the problem is more drastic than that," he said on a sigh, running a hand through his hair. "They sent official notice to the academy and the sector that they're coming here to meet with the staff."

"Your family—"

"Not really my family," Clanguard countered, "which is why I'm warning you. It's representatives from several different groups in the city, including the aquatic shifters. They want assurances that this isn't going to be breeding grounds for an alliance of the four clans because all of you are mates."

"And how the hell would we prove that? It's an unintentional alliance," Breaker growled.

"Is the headmistress okay with this?" Jagger questioned, looking angry.

"She's been preoccupied with other things, so while she's aware of it, we'll be handling it internally," he said. "We're hoping to ease their minds about it, which is where all of you come in. The meeting is tonight."

"And you want us to do what?" Gage said, throwing his hands in the air. "Come and coddle them? Tell them that everything will be okay?" Then before Clanguard could answer, he tacked on, "Were our parents made aware of this meeting?"

"No," Clanguard admitted. "Well, not officially. I've made them aware the same as I'm making you aware and asking you to aid in our endeavor. The last thing we need is groups of paranoid shifters outside of the academy. It'll only multiply when their children bring it into these walls, and it'll make everything ten times harder."

"We aren't going to say anything that would be helpful," Jagger said. "We *are* going to be an alliance. The four clans are going to be brought together in some shape or form, there's no way around that. Bexley is our mate."

"I think if you show up and show that you aren't

combative, or explain that you aren't trying to plan anything—"

"I don't understand why they're so worried," I finally spoke up, drawing everyone's attention. "If the clans already rule everything outside of the sector and the rogue lands, why would it matter to them? Worst situation would be us combining clan lands, right?"

"Their fear is that you would come for the city next," Clanguard explained. "That has always been my family's fear. They're so concerned about keeping their pack as pure and powerful as possible that they view any other ruling creatures as a potential threat. They've never been strong enough to stand against the dragon clans, though, so I imagine this is their way of 'fighting back.' Instead of directly confronting your parents, they're going to try to prey on this situation."

"You recognize this is bullshit," Breaker rumbled.

"Of course I do," Clanguard bit out. "I'm letting you know for precisely that reason. If you come to the meeting, they will have no reason to push the issue further. Your presence will show a willingness for open communication, which the other groups will see. Following that, your parents can handle it on the outside."

Silence filled the room as I considered his words.

"I don't know a lot about shifter politics, but I prefer to stay out of them," I admitted.

"You don't have to change that," Gage promised. "We can ignore this."

"But," I drew out, "I think we should go. Professor Clanguard is right—it could eliminate tension, and if we don't go, their anger is guaranteed. I don't want your parents to have to deal with the fallout of my presence here."

"They won't view it that way," Jagger countered.

I met each of their eyes and tried to put as much resolve as possible into my words. My instincts were telling me it was the right move. "I think it's a good idea to go."

"Then we'll go." Gage stood. "What time?"

"Two hours from now in the west conference room," Clanguard said, stepping back and offering all of us a thankful look. "I think this really will help things. I'll see you there."

I watched as he stepped into the elevator and the doors closed, his words leaving me feeling conflicted. I believed that it would help things, I really did—that was why I wanted to go—but now I was second-guessing myself. What if it didn't help? What if it made it worse? What if they viewed us as being combative?

It seemed to be a common thread throughout

shifter society, and if any level of aggression was perceived... Well, usually it escalated to an extreme extent. I wanted to believe that tonight wouldn't result in that, but I just didn't know.

Jagger Silvershade

I could practically feel the nervous tension rolling off my little treasure, and I so badly wanted to fix this for her. To assure her that everything would be okay because I knew that it would be. I wasn't concerned about the threat that these other parties involved posed—we out-powered them even on a bad day. But it wasn't about raw power and strength to Bexley. It was about making sure that no one got hurt in any way, that no one was having to go through more trouble than needed.

The woman was so damn considerate that it sometimes hurt. It was one of many things that I loved about her.

Love. It wasn't a hard word to consider when it came to Bexley, and as I watched her take her time getting ready, meticulously curling her hair and choosing an outfit, I fought the urge to pick her brain. To demand that she tell me every little thing she was thinking about, every little thing she was worried about.

I wanted to solve all of it.

"Is this okay?" She held up a silver sweater and a black leather skirt, her brows knitted together. "Or should I wear something nicer? I literally have no idea. Maybe I can call Celine—"

"Bexley." I took her face between my hands and pressed a kiss to her lips. "You look beautiful no matter what you wear. Do not overthink this. We're only going in an effort to play nice. At the end of the day, they don't matter, and if they try to cause a problem, they're going to very quickly see how fast we'll end it."

"It's true," Gage said from the doorway. "Clanguard may be viewing us as the children of the clan leaders, but most of the reins and powers have been passed to us throughout the past year or two, so if we need to make a call, we can do that. I won't hesitate to protect our families—none of us will—and if they present a threat, even a small one, and don't back down..."

Bexley nodded in understanding, her eyes shaded with sadness. "I don't want it to come to that."

"I don't think it will," Breaker said from where he sat on her bed, leaning forward with his elbows on his knees. "I think the others have been manipulated to feel scared of a threat that doesn't exist. We have no interest in the city. I think the people who are instigating all of this are the Clanguard family—they're the true problem."

Bexley exhaled. "And Professor Clanguard doesn't seem to associate himself with his family? Like at all?"

"No one knows the full story," I answered, "but apparently it's been years since he's spoken with anyone other than his brother. I believe the conflict started with him deciding to teach here...or maybe it was the result of their fight... Either way, he has completely disowned his family."

"And no one knows why?" She frowned.

"I have to assume it's due to their purist beliefs. As a professor who teaches all different types of shifters, it would be hard to be like that, and it's clear to me, at least, that he isn't," I explained.

"You're right, that would be hard," she whispered. "I feel bad for him, and I hope that it doesn't result in Rachel getting caught up in anything dangerous."

"I think as long as she doesn't go to their pack lands, she should be fine," Breaker stated quietly. I offered him a look because I wasn't positive I believed that. The Clanguards were notorious for being dangerous. It was why when Gage realized Bexley was friends with Fletcher, he'd been especially worked up about it. They weren't a group of people you wanted around your loved ones, especially your fucking mate.

I wasn't positive how true it was, but a long time ago I heard rumors that the women in their pack were treated like slaves. That they had no rights. No freedoms. I hadn't heard that rumor in a long time, and I knew that if it had been true to any extent, our parents would have stepped in... But that rumor had most likely stemmed from a seed of truth, and I didn't trust that a mentality like that would just fade.

"Alright," Bexley said, satisfied for the moment. "I'm going to get dressed, and then we can leave."

Seconds later, the bathroom door shut, and I looked at both men in the room before saying, "We need to be prepared to confront the Clanguards on the outside if this escalates. They acted way too fast for this to not have been planned. I mean, to get this many families riled up after the announcement was made less than two days ago?"

"You're right," Breaker said, his gaze darkening. "He already let the parents know so they'll be on standby, but if tonight doesn't go well, I think we need to consider leaving a message that they'll better understand."

"They may view it as the start of a war," Gage murmured in thought.

"That would be suicidal," I growled. "They may have a large pack, but against three dragon clans? You'd have to be crazy."

"You've heard the rumors," Gage said. "Who the hell knows what they're willing to do if they are so damn paranoid."

The bathroom door opened as Bexley walked back into her bedroom, slipping on a pair of earrings. I nearly groaned as she put on ankle boots, her long legs drawing my attention as she hummed a song under her breath, oblivious to how we were all fucking staring at her. I had no idea how Bexley didn't realize how fucking perfect she was, but if I needed to tell her for the rest of our lives, then it would be an honor.

"Alright." She offered me a small nervous smile. "Let's do this."

Nodding, I stood up and led her from the room. Breaker and Gage had managed to find two additional umbrellas, which would make it a lot easier than having to sprint from building to building.

"Wait." She nibbled her lip. "It's storming—do we need to worry about our magic?"

"They're older, which means they should be more controlled," I explained. "It may make them uncomfortable, but other than that, they should be fine."

The answer seemed to suffice as we left the dorms and walked towards the academic building, the rain pattering down on our umbrella. Campus seemed particularly quiet this evening, and I knew it was partly the weather, but I also had a feeling people could tell there was tension in the air. Shifters were good at sensing danger like that, and older, more powerful shifters on campus would result in that exact sensation.

When we finally got inside and put down the umbrellas, Gage led us towards the west wing of the academic building. The large conference rooms weren't used very often—only in the case of club or group meetings—but it made sense for this. What didn't make sense was why the Clanguard family hadn't gone directly to our families. I had to trust the professor on this and assume it was an intimidation tactic.

Something that was nearly laughable.

Voices greeted us as we walked into a large room filled with professors as well as older women and men, around twenty people in total. Professor Clanguard was at the door, and upon seeing us, he visibly relaxed.

"Thank you for joining us," he said easily.

"Everyone is here, so feel free to take a seat up front. Hopefully this will be over fairly quickly."

I had a feeling that his wish would *not* come to fruition.

My gaze instantly moved over the crowd, snagging on someone who looked a lot like Fletcher but older with silver hair. His eyes were narrowed on us, his jaw tight, and malice radiated off of him, but his attention was specifically focused on the woman next to me. When I looked down at her, hoping to keep her attention from him, she was already staring.

"Bex." I drew her chin up as her gaze darted from him and back to me. Her eyes were filled with shadows, and her brows knitted in confusion. "What's wrong?"

"Who is that?" she whispered. Her hands had started trembling. "I think... I think I know him. But I don't know how."

"That's Linan Clanguard."

Like an electric bolt hit her, horror washed across Bexley's face, her skin turning white as paper as her grip on me tightened. Panic hit me as her eyes closed, tears leaking down her cheeks.

Fuck. What the—

"Jagger," she whispered, her voice barely audible. "That's the name. That's the name from the memory. I think...I think that's the man who killed my family."

Surge (Book 3) - Available for order!

Interested in the other DIA students?
    Deva's story - Order here!
    Alexandra's story - Order here!
    Alina's story - Order here!

Love Bexley?

Come meet Effie at SFU!

Lost: Silver Falls University (Book One)
Preview on the next page!

Five broken alphas. One lost wolf. A fate she never expected.

Silver Falls University. There was no reason for a female bitten wolf like myself to be here. More so, there was no reason that someone who grew up as poor as I did, in an overcrowded pack-house in the South Side of Chicago, should be making her way up north to one of the most prestigious supernatural universities in the country. I truly had no idea what to expect. Something that was my own fault. I didn't exactly have a lot of experience with anyone or anything. 'Sheltered' was an understatement, except to the darkness that came with struggling to survive cruel bullying and incurable loneliness that had formed the woman I was today. The place I had grown up never felt like home. No one had ever felt like home. Well, until I met a man on the way to campus. A man that had me feeling so completely comfortable, yet confused and overwhelmed. There had to be something wrong with me, right? This wasn't normal. Then again, I should have realized that nothing about my life moving forward would be normal. I just didn't realize how much was in store for me.

Join Effie Harlow on her journey at Silver Falls University, where she begins to realize that something about her is different. This slow-burn reverse harem paranormal romance features five protective and possessive shifter mates that are bound and determined to keep Effie by their side, no matter what. To prove to her that she is so much more than anyone has ever tried to tell her she was. Will they be able to convince her of her place at Silver Falls and in their life? Or will Effie get lost in the university crowds like she did back home?

Find out in this first installment of five in the Silver Falls University Series. Warning: This PNR university-style RH will contain swearing, adult sexual content +18, elements of PTSD and mention of prior emotional, sexual, and physical abuse, violence, and additional darker themes. Mild cliff-hanger warning - the 2nd installment of the Silver Falls University series, Forgotten, is now available for pre-order.

Lost: Silver Falls University

Chapter One Preview - Effie Harlow

"Next stop—*Kirkwall*."

My quiet humming momentarily cut off as I winced. The overhead intercom's static interference made it nearly impossible to hear which stop we were arriving at. My ears rang uncomfortably as my wolf shifted under my skin, offering me a frustrated look. As if this was somehow my fault!

Luckily, I had heard enough to distinguish the word 'Kirkwall,' meaning that I was nearly to my stop. From what I understood about this train system, there was little to no chance of missing the stop since it was quite literally the end of the line. At least, I hoped my understanding was correct. The last thing I needed today, considering I barely had enough money to make it onto campus, was dealing with more train fares and schedules.

My humming once again picked up as I refocused on the southern Wisconsin town that I was now traveling through. This was the furthest I'd ever been from home. Something that was both intimidating and exciting.

This was a good thing.

That was what I continued to tell myself, because if I didn't, I was liable to freak out, considering the massive change that I was embarking on. Completely alone, mind you. A change that I hadn't exactly willingly volunteered for, either.

No, none of this, as with most things in my life, had been my choice. I had never considered moving anywhere, let alone three hours north of my South Side Chicago home. More so, the concept of attending a university of any kind, especially one like this, had never crossed my mind. *Why would it?* I may have been sheltered from the world outside of our pack, but I knew enough to understand that girls like me didn't get the opportunity to further their education past high school.

Girls like me worked at their pack's local bar as a waitress and lived with their parents until they managed to attract a mate and pop out their own litter of wolves. Appealing, right? But despite its unsavory nature to me, I had accepted that was my future. *Or I had assumed so.*

Now, though? Well, now I felt far more free to accept just how much that concept had truly bothered me. I knew mating was necessary to continuing a pack's heritage and family line, but it had never sounded like something I wanted to take part in. My nose scrunched slightly as I considered the concept of mating with any of the boys that I knew from back home. *No. No, thank you.*

Was it normal to feel so distasteful about men in general?

Actually, that was a lie. Most men didn't bother me at all... until they showed themselves to be similar to the man that took me in, Gerald. When those qualities—quick to temper and general disdain for all females—showed themselves, I usually found myself completely disenchanted.

Not that I'd ever been 'enchanted' with a man to begin with, if we were being honest. I may have found them attractive at first, but upon hearing their cruel language and watching how they treated others? Any attraction had completely disappeared.

Fertility and strength of your mate.

Theresa, Gerald's wife, and her friends constantly claimed that the 'fertility and strength of your mate' was far more important than the substance. Something that not only left me with an uneasy feeling in my stomach, but didn't ring true. I was positive they believed what they were saying, but I felt like that was more of a lie created to make shifter women think they were happy or content with the mates they had, even if the pairing was far from perfect. Once coming to that realization, my disdain for relationships like that had only grown further.

Relationships where your opinion wasn't respected.

Relationships where you were blamed entirely for not being able to produce pups.

Relationships where you were essentially a servant in your own home.

I may have been a more quiet individual, but I was far from ignorant. Rather the opposite, and I found myself constantly wanting to stand up for her against Gerald. What went on between the man and woman I had lived with was far from normal, even if it was accepted in our pack. I'd learned my lesson, though—it was far safer to keep my opinions to myself.

I knew, bone deep, that how he treated her wasn't right.

I knew the bruises he left on her and me weren't acceptable.

I knew the hatred he spewed about how she

looked and acted was why she constantly appeared withdrawn and exhausted.

Yet when I tried to intervene at all, even talking to her in private, I was somehow the one at fault. I was either 'too young to understand' or 'ungrateful to the man that provided a roof over our head.' The latter was not even factual, because Gerald didn't have a job, so Alpha technically owned our apartment. But that didn't matter. Theresa had twisted it in her head so that those elements weren't important and that they were minor inconveniences that 'us women' had to deal with.

After all, *you know how men can be.*

I hated that phrase. I had heard it time and time again, making my frustration with the situation grow and turn into a general wariness about mating as a whole. Something that should have been impossible, considering I was a wolf shifter and mating was literally second nature to us. But... maybe it wasn't mating that upset me as much as the concept of being with someone like Gerald.

Why couldn't your mate be expected to treat you with respect? I knew I was supposed to be submissive by nature, not only as a female shifter but as the type of wolf I was, but everything told me that we weren't meant to be treated like that.

Relief flooded me as I realized what a bullet I'd

dodged. I had truly believed that my only option was for me to mate with someone like that, and now that it wasn't my unavoidable future? I was both angry at myself for having accepted that fate so easily and also a bit terrified because I had absolutely no idea what my future would hold. It couldn't be worse than what I would have been going through, though, right? I was praying to the Goddess that was the case.

My fists tightened slightly, nails digging into my palms, as a thread of anxiety began to unravel in my abdomen. Change was not my friend, and there was absolutely no way to avoid it, considering my life was being turned upside down. I was being thrust into a new world, almost literally, and expected to make my way into it with ease? That seemed unfair.

I craved stability. I craved to understand and be able to predict what would come next in my daily life, and right now I couldn't even tell you where my next meal was coming from. While I knew this change could yield positive results, I was still cautious, because everything about this situation was far from my normal. That didn't even include all the unanswered questions I had.

First of all, how was I even headed to this university in the first place? Why could no one answer that simple question for me? I mean, my grades were decent, but... It made absolutely no sense.

Silver Falls University.

When Gerald and Theresa had informed me about my 'change of plans' a few days ago, I'd thought they were teasing me. They had to be joking, right? I mean, why else would they state it so casually? The only thing that convinced me was when they'd handed me the acceptance letter to a university that I knew I had never applied to.

In fact, I had never bothered applying to any colleges following my graduation the previous spring. No one from my graduating class, with the exception of two students, had chosen to go to university this past fall. It just wasn't something any of us did. Not only because of the financial hardship it put on the pack, but because, as I said, there wasn't a lot of emphasis on education overall.

So who had submitted my information for a late start in the spring semester? That was one more question that no one seemed to be able to articulate an answer for. Then again, I didn't push it very much, especially since we had been surrounded by so many other pack members the past few days, everyone seemingly shocked at the change of fortune.

Despite my unease with change, it was getting me out of a toxic situation. Plus, I'd been awarded a full scholarship, so I would owe my pack and the school nothing.

Do you know how much it took for someone to want to get away from a pack that saved their life? To not want to feel indebted to the people that brought me in when I was cold and stumbling through the streets? A lot. Trust me when I said there were a hundred reasons why I'd needed to get out of there, and half of them had to do with the current bruising on my body.

I healed faster than a human but slower than most wolf shifters. So when a full-grown male wolf shifter like Gerald served out a hit or two? You better believe that it didn't heal right away. Despite Theresa seeming to accept the mistreatment that I knew was wrong, I would take any way out of such a toxic situation. When I'd been presented with an opportunity, I'd leapt at it.

A mysterious scholarship to one of the most prestigious universities in the Midwest was not something I was going to question. Especially if no one else was. Something that I should have found suspicious, but at the time I'd been just wanting an escape. Now though, as I sat on this train overthinking the massive change I was making, the unease and anxiety was making itself known once again.

Had they truly wanted me gone that bad? Was that why they had jumped on it? I hadn't thought I was that much of a problem, considering I normally kept to myself.

More so, was this a bad idea?

Or a dangerous situation?

Want more? Pick up Lost today!

Lost: Silver Falls University (Book One)

Series Within DIA Universe

Monarchs of Hell (Completed Series) by R.L. Caulder and M. Sinclair
    Insurrection: mybook.to/Monarchs1
    Imbalance: mybook.to/Monarchs2
    Inheritance: mybook.to/Monarchs3

Dark Imaginarium Academy Series
    Phases of the Moon by M. Sinclair
    The Creatures We Crave by R.L. Caulder
    The Storm Dragons' Mate by M. Sinclair
    Blood Oath by R.L. Caulder

M. Sinclair

USA Today Bestselling Author

M. Sinclair is a Chicago native, parent to 3 cats, and can be found writing almost every moment of the day. Despite being new to publishing, M. Sinclair has been writing for nearly 10 years now. Currently in love with the Reverse Harem genre, she plans to publish an array of works that are considered romance, suspense, and horror within the year. M. Sinclair lives by the notion that there is enough room for all types of heroines in this world, and being saved is as important as saving others. If you love fantasy romance, obsessive possessive alpha males, and tough FMCs, then M. Sinclair is for you!

Published Works

M. Sinclair has crafted different universes with unique plotlines, character cameos, and shared universe events. As a reader, this means that you may see your favorite character or characters... appear in multiple books besides their own storyline.

Universe 1

Established in 2019

VENGEANCE

Book 1 - Savages

Book 2 - Lunatics

Book 3 - Monsters

Book 4 - Psychos

Complete Series

Vengeance : The Complete Series

THE RED MASQUES

Book 1 - Raven Blood

Book 2 - Ashes & Bones

Book 3 - Shadow Glass

Book 4 - Fire & Smoke

Book 5 - Dark King

Complete Series

A Raven Masques Novel - Birth of a Raven

TEARS OF THE SIREN

Book 1 - Horror of Your Heart

Book 2 - Broken House

Book 3 - Neon Drops

Book 4 - Snapped Strings

Book 5 - Fractured Souls

DESCENDANT

Book 1 - Descendant of Chaos

Book 2 - Descendant of Blood

Book 3 - Descendant of Sin

Book 4 - Descendant of Glory

Book 5 - Descendant of Pain

Book 6 - Descendant of Victory

REBORN

Book 1 - Reborn In Flames

Book 2 - Soaring In Flames

Book 3 - Realm Of Flames

Book 4 - Dying in Flames

Book 5 - Ruling in Flames

Complete Series

THE WRONGED

Book 1 - Wicked Blaze Correctional

Book 2 - Evading Wicked Blaze

Book 3 - Defeating Wicked Blaze

Complete Series

LOST IN FAE

Book 1 - Finding Fae

Book 2 - Exploring Fae

Book 3 - Freeing Fae

Universe 2

Established in 2020

AMONG SHADOWS

Book 1 - Court of Betrayal

Book 2 - Court of Deception

* * *

Paranormal & Fantasy Series

THESE SERIES ARE NOT CURRENTLY AFFILIATED WITH A SPECIFIC M. SINCLAIR UNIVERSE.

PHASES OF THE MOON

Book 1 - Lunar Witch

Book 2 - Blood Witch

Book 3 - Shadow Witch

Book 4 - TBA

THE STORM DRAGONS' MATE

Book 1 - Blitz

Book 2 - Flicker

Book 3 - Surge

Book 4 - TBA

THE DEAD AND NOT SO DEAD

Book 1 - Queen of the Dead

Book 2 - Team Time with the Dead

Book 3 - Dying for the Dead

Complete Series

Complete Collection: The Shadows of Wildberry Lane

THEIR POSSESSION

Book 1 - Sheltered

Book 2 - Searched

* * *

Standalone Novels

Peridot (Jewels Cafe Series)

Time for Sensibility (Women of Time)

WILLOWDALE VILLAGE COLLECTION

A collection of standalone novels about the women of Willowdale Village.

Voiceless

SEASONS OF THE HUNTRESS

Winter Huntress

* * *

Collaborations

MONARCHS OF HELL

(M. Sinclair & R.L. Caulder)

Book 1 - Insurrection

Book 2 - Imbalance

Book 3 - Inheritance

Completed series

The Vampyres' Source

(M. Sinclair & R.L. Caulder)

Book 1 - Ruthless Blood

Book 2 - Ruthless War

Book 3 - Ruthless Love

Rebel Hearts Heists Duet

(M. Sinclair & Melissa Adams)

Book 1 - Steal Me

Book 2 - Keep Me

Completed Duet

Forbidden Fairytales

(The Grim Sisters - M. Sinclair & CY Jones)

Book 1 - Stolen Hood

Book 2 - Knights of Sin

Book 3 - Deadly Games

Made in the USA
Columbia, SC
01 July 2024

37962763R00200